They Do Not Exist

Stories from the Human Defence Unit Book One

Iris Carden

Published by: Iris Carden
              Ipswich, Qld, Australia
              iriscardenauthor.net
ISBN: 978-0-6459679-4-4
Cover art: Full Moon City by Iris Carden
A catalogue record for this work is available from the National
Library of Australia.
This book is the product of human, not artificial, intelligence.

Stories

Introduction

Five storeys below Brisbane's Roma Street Police Station, is the headquarters for the Human Defence Unit. Its members are drawn from among the highest performing members of military, intelligence, and police forces throughout Australia, along with select highly specialised members of the civilian population. The Human Defence Unit and its elite staff are neither police, military nor intelligence. They do not exist.

They Do Not Exist

Senior Agent Jo Burns read the email alert, sent from the police station five storeys above her head. Three victims, all with neck wounds, all exsanguinated. She replied with instructions for the bodies to be moved to the HDU mortuary, and the police investigation to cease immediately.

She decided to take the new guy with her, and called Trainee Agent Harry Smythe.

"Vampires," she said. "What weapons do you need?"

"UV laser pointer, gun with silver bullets."

"No. Silver bullets are for werewolves. You want the mini-crossbow. Wooden stakes, but be sure to get the heart. A machete is useful as well, to remove the head, but that's harder to carry. Gear up, and make sure you've checked the batteries in your laser pointer. We're going upstairs in five minutes."

While Harry was getting his gear organised, Jo called Helen Thompson, the unit's pathologist. "Three suspected fang victims coming down for you. Don't know their condition or if they're likely to turn."

"I'll stay ready to hit the UV lights just in case," Helen was matter-of-fact, despite having come close to being werewolf lunch only the previous week.

Jo and Harry went first to the office of Inspector David Webber, their Queensland Police contact. He gave them the details police had already gathered.

The three women had shared a flat in a multi-storey building adjacent Roma Street Parklands. A co-worker of one of the women had gone to check after she had been absent work. A member of the building security staff had attempted to get a response from the women, and then had used a master key to access the flat, where he'd found the three bodies in their beds.

Forensics had begun their inspection of the scene, but that had now been stopped. Jo ordered HDU forensics and clean-up unit to take over.

"What do you think we do now?" Jo asked Harry.

"We question the co-worker, and the building security guy?"

"No. We don't draw attention to our investigation. Fangs hunt close to home. We're looking for someone who lives close to the victims, probably in the same building, who never goes out during the day. A good indicator for vamps in the city is the extremes they go to in avoiding daylight. It will be someone who works from home, or works nights, and who had some extreme blockout curtains or metal rollerblinds. You're driving."

While Harry drove to the apartment building, Jo worked on her laptop computer from the passenger seat.

"Three people in the apartment building work from home, cross-referenced with satellite photos of the building, we have one candidate. Henrietta Dix, who has aluminium roller blinds on all exterior windows. She owns her own flat, so she can make those kind of changes. Her personal wealth is multiple millions, in shares and savings, not in line with her editing job. She's been saving over several lifetimes."

"How do you get all that information like that? Like you've just accessed satellite photos, tax records, what?"

"Yes and yes, and a number of other, not-quite-so-legal resources. We don't exist and we're not constrained by the law. You'll learn how to access our sources as you go on. Just go straight to the parking garage."

"It's residents only."

Jo passed him a card. "Open Sesame," she said.

Harry tapped the card to the card reader, and to his surprise, the gate opened.

On the tenth floor, Jo led the way to the suspect's flat. She knocked on the door. There was no answer. "Henrietta Dix, open the door. Police," Jo said.

"But we're not police," Harry whispered.

The door still did not open. Jo pulled a lock picking kit from her pocket and opened the door.

"She's hiding. Stay by the door in case she tries to escape," Jo instructed.

She began her systematic search of all possible hiding places. Eventually she opened a guest room wardrobe, to find a tall, middle-aged woman, hiding there.

"Henrietta," Jo said, "been snacking on any neighbours lately?"

The woman snarled, drawing her lips back to reveal fangs.

Jo pressed the mini-crossbow's wooden bolt into the woman's chest as she pulled the trigger.

The vampire slumped, falling to the floor.

Jo was almost at the door, when Harry, still waiting there, aimed his laser pointer over her left shoulder.

Jo heard the yell, as the second vampire had the pinpoint of artificial sunlight directly in his face. The fang pulled back, as Jo turned to face him. She shot a wooden bolt through his heart.

"Thanks," she said.

"That was a real vampire," Harry was shaken.

"We don't bother hunting pretend ones," Jo replied.

Krampus

Trainee Agent Harry Smythe put a small decorated Christmas tree and a model Santa on his desk.

Agent Marissa Tyler, walking past, stopped and said, "Put the Santa away before Jo sees it. She'll go ballistic."

"But it's just Christmas stuff. Is this a religious thing or something?"

"No, it's a kidnapping and murder thing."

"A what?"

"Do you know Jo's story?"

"She was a cop, wasn't she?"

Marissa sighed. "I don't know if I should tell you this, but you've met David Webber, the police inspector? He's our contact in the police station."

"Yes, I've met him."

"He and Jo used to be married. They broke up after their little girl Katie was kidnapped and murdered. The offender was a Krampus."

"A Krampus? Like a bad Santa?"

"Exactly like a bad Santa. Santas and Krampus are the same species. They turn for a week around the start of December each year, around Saint Nicholas' day."

"So how are Santa and Saint Nicholas are related?"

"They turn at the same time of year as he died. That's the relationship. Anyway, they have a good year, and think of happy things and what they're grateful for, they become a Santa, and they're compelled to give little gifts to people around them, especially children. They have a bad year, collect up resentments and grudges, they turn into Krampus and are compelled to abuse and assault the people around them."

"Santa exists, but it's not Saint Nicholas, and there's not just one of them. And Santa and evil Santa are the same thing. Got it. I never expected that."

"You're OK with fangs and wolves, but not Santas and Krampus? Wait till you find out about Christmas ghosts."

"What?"

"Back to my story. This particular Krampus was a nasty piece of work even as a human. Lots of priors for minor assaults, drunk and disorderly, petty theft, dealing, all the low-level crimes that end up growing into big stuff. Jo was still a cop then. She'd arrested him multiple times during the year. David had arrested him once or twice as well. When he turned, he had two targets for revenge, and one way to devastate them both simultaneously."

"Little Katie?"

"Little Katie. Actually her whole daycare group."

"Did they catch him?"

"It was Jo's day to pick up Katie from daycare. When she found the kids gone, she tracked that Krampus and killed it. She saved all the other kids but little Katie didn't make it."

"You're kidding."

"Nup. I was a trainee agent back then. I was working alongside Kurt Davison, who was Senior Agent before Jo. That guy was a legend. Remind me one day to tell you about how he brought in the Bundamba Yowie. That wasn't a huge fight or anything, but took more patience than anything I've ever seen. Anyway, when Kurt saw how well Jo had handled the Krampus, he offered her a job here. Well, that's the story. That's why we don't have Santas around here. You can leave up your Christmas tree, but ditch the Santa before Jo sees it."

Harry picked up his model Santa. In minutes, it had gone from a whimsical symbol of the season to being something sinister. He dropped it in the waste paper bin under his desk.

Techno Ghost

Senior Agent Jo Burns called Trainee Agent Harry Smythe to her office. As always, she quizzed him about his knowledge on the subject before taking him on assignment.

"What do you know about ghosts, Harry?"

"Most ghosts are deceased humans with unfinished business. Poltergeists are the outworking of living humans emotions in turmoil, usually teenagers."

"Leaving poltergeists aside, how do we resolve a haunting?"

"Exorcism?"

"That's demonic possession. We communicate with the ghost, and we assist in resolving its unfinished business."

"How do we do that? Ouija board?"

"Sometimes." She held up a small USB stick. "In this case, an electronic ouija board, invented by the German equivalent of the HDU. We're visiting a major company, where all of the computer monitors keep showing the outline of a human face, and have been for about a week. We're presenting ourselves as a specialist IT team, brought in to fix the problem."

In offices of McMahon and Associates, the agents were given access to a terminal in the business server room. On the screen in front of them were faint outlines of eyes and a mouth, opened in a scream. Jo plugged the USB into the drive, and typed: "How can I help you?"

On the screen, very faint, and appearing to be handwritten, appeared the words: "Find me. Find my killer."

Jo typed, "Can you give me details?"

No further words appeared on the screen. "They don't have enough energy for more than that, or maybe they don't know," Jo explained to Harry.

"So what now?"

"Let's meet the CEO."

Jim McMahon was a large man, who looked like a heart attack waiting to happen.

"We need to know if someone has left the company suddenly, maybe around the time the face appeared."

"You think it's sabotage?" the fat man asked.

"I think if you have an employee who has left or gone missing, they might be able to help me fix the problem."

"One of our IT people, Liz Jones, didn't show up to work on Monday, no explanation. We haven't heard from her since. The face appeared on Monday morning. I'll have someone get you her contact details. Honestly, Liz is a good worker, we were stunned she just ghosted us, and I can't think of any reason she would do this."

Jo knocked at the door of the woman's house. As expected there was no answer. Jo used her lock pick kit. Inside, the house was in disarray, and the smell of decomposition was overwhelming.

"I guess we found her," Harry said. "Now we have to find her killer."

"Definitely explains why she ghosted her work."

Jo found the woman's mobile phone, and used her Open Sesame card to unlock it.

"Isn't that what you used to open that parking garage last week? And how many laws have we just broken?" Harry asked.

"It opens practically any kind of electronic lock, and we haven't broken any laws because we're not here," she answered, as she searched the phone.

"Liz was being harassed by a coworker. Looks like Mick was her direct supervisor. She's turned him down politely, and then more forcefully, but he wouldn't give up. His last texts were just spewing hatred. We're calling David Webber to get police and forensics here to be sure, but it looks like Mick's going to jail, and Liz can move on."

They went back to McMahon and associates. Jo plugged the USB into the computer again. "I found you. Mick is about to be arrested. Rest in peace."

The face disappeared from the screen.

Wolf

Senior Agent Jo Burns had been called to the office of Inspector David Webber, the police liaison with the HDU. She was surprised to find the Queensland Premier already in the office, waiting for her.

The Premier passed a manila file folder, labelled "confidential", to Jo. "Do you know who this is?" she asked.

Jo opened the file to the first page, which had a photo and a name. "He's a misogynist, who calls himself a men's rights activist and argues publicly for the right of men to beat women. He's touring now, and women are protesting outside all his venues."

"He's missing," the Premier said.

"I hope he stays that way," Jo replied.

The Premier pushed a stray hair back behind her ear. "I share your sentiment, but he's high profile and he's gone missing in Brisbane. It's not a good look for the state, or the city. Read through the file, you'll see why I wanted you."

Jo looked through the file. The door to the man's hotel room had been broken open forcefully, and there were claw marks on both the door and the door jamb. There was very little else damaged.

"Wolf," Jo said, "one with a lot of self-control, so probably hereditary, not created. I see there's hair in the evidence log. David, can you transfer that to Helen Thompson in our pathology section. She can run DNA and see if the wolf's on our register."

"You have a register?" the Premier asked. "Don't you just kill these things?"

"Not every monster behaves monstrously. Some have self-control and choose not to harm humans. Fangs can get blood from the blood bank. Blood that's diseased or contaminated isn't suitable for human transfusions, goes on the fang market. Wolves sometimes choose to lock or chain themselves up for the full moon. Those we know of who stay out of trouble are on our DNA register. Sometimes they need help to stay out of trouble. On the full moon, we have a number of wolves present themselves to go into our cells because they don't have someone to lock them up at home."

"Just find him and deal with the offender," the Premier said.

"Oh, I will, but do you want to be advised of the results? I mean if he's already wolf scat, that's not really going to reflect well on the state either."

The DNA test had a positive result. Tegan Morris was a wolf who in her human form ran a small florist shop, and lived in a house behind the shop.

The florist put down the flowers she was arranging when she saw Jo arrive. "I've been expecting you," she said. "I was going to kill him, but I couldn't go through with it."

She led Jo to a soundproofed, basement room below her house. In the middle of the room was a large steel cage. Inside the cage, sitting on the bare floor was the missing man.

"This is where you usually stay when you turn?" Jo asked.

"Yes, my sister usually locks me in. She didn't inherit the werewolf gene. She died two weeks ago. Her husband beat her to death after reading this man's blog."

"Unlock the door," Jo said.

"Are you arresting me?"

"No. You didn't harm him, and you're not going to do anything like this again, are you?"

"I don't want to, but I don't have anyone to lock me in."

"I'll do it. You can be locked into our cells, or I'll come and lock you in here. Now you need to let him out."

"But he'll tell people what happened."

"He was kidnapped by a werewolf. Yes. He can tell anyone he likes, that's not going to be taken seriously." She turned to the man in the cell. "Get up. You're coming with me."

"You're the police?" the prisoner asked.

"No."

"Then why should I come with you?"

Tegan opened the door, and Jo grabbed the man and dragged him out of the cell. "Because you've got an appointment with the Premier. I'm going to drop you off at her office and hopefully never have to think of you again."

"If you're not the police, who are you?"

"No-one. I don't exist."

"You what?"

"You're hallucinating. Police found you wandering around Fortitude Valley ranting about werewolves. You really should quit taking drugs."

"That's not true."

"That's what the police report that's going to accidentally be leaked to the press will say. Push your luck, and you'll be arrested for using."

"I'm going to report you."

"Report who? To whom? As I said, I don't exist."

Vigilante

The cage was in a basement room, under an otherwise ordinary house.

Senior Agent Jo Burns noticed the marks where a cutting tool had been used to remove the door. On the floor, she saw a large pool of blood, and the basement walls were sprayed with blood. On the outside of the cage, an oxy-acetylene torch lay with the removed door.

"What is this place?" Trainee Agent Harry Smythe asked.

"Wolf cage," Jo replied. "Wolves who want to be responsible people have someone lock them in their cage on the full moon, so they're confined while they turn."

"So what happened? Did the wolf kill someone? Or what?"

"Notice the door to the cage was removed with that cutting tool. Someone was actually stupid enough to break into a wolf cage, during the full moon."

"How can you be sure the wolf was in here?"

Jo sighed. "I locked her in myself, after work yesterday. The person who normally locked her in had died. She had no-one else, so I did it for her."

"So someone broke in and…"

"And either they killed the wolf, or the wolf killed them. Helen will tell us which."

Pathologist Helen Thompson was at that moment doing a field test on the blood, she'd already photographed, measured, dusted for fingerprints and performed all of the other arcane mysteries of forensics units everywhere.

Helen looked up from her test, "It's a mix. Human and wolf, in surprisingly even amounts. I'd say they were both seriously injured, but given wolves' propensity for healing it's more likely than the human to still be alive."

"How do we find the killer wolf?"

"First, we don't jump to conclusions. Second, we check the hospitals. She's turned back by now and must need medical attention. Even with a wolf's propensity for healing, she was clearly seriously injured. We start with hospitals. We'll find her and talk to her and find out her story. In the meantime, Helen will run DNA, forensics will run fingerprints, and we'll hope to find out who the human involved was."

A check of hospitals located Tegan Morris, full-time self-employed florist, and part-time werewolf. She was seriously injured, recovering from multiple stab wounds.

Morris gave a pained half-smile as Jo and Harry entered her room. "Did I kill him, Agent Burns?" she asked.

"We don't know yet, Tegan. Can you tell me what happened."

"Just after you left, this man just walked into the basement. I guess he must have broken into the house after you locked it. He was prepared, said he knew what I was. He had a cutting tool, an oxy torch, I think it's called. He cut through the hinges and lock on the cage door, and came in, with a knife. It was silver, so I didn't heal straight away when I turned. He had me cornered and was stabbing me, I was yelling, hoping you were still near enough to hear. Then I turned, and I don't know what happened. I woke up in the park across the road from my shop. I was under some bushes, I think I crawled in there. You know, how animals crawl away and hide to die? When I woke up, I was sure I was going to die. Then a woman walking her dog found me and called an ambulance."

"You don't know what happened between when you turned and when you woke up?"

"Just flashes. Darkness, the smell of blood. Ripping, tearing, whether it was me ripping him, or his knife stabbing me, I'm not sure. Sorry, I can't help more than that. I hope I didn't kill him, but if I did, it was because he attacked me."

"That's pretty much the story the scene told me," Jo said. "Did you recognise him? Was he known to you?"

She shook her head.

"Get some rest. We'll talk again."

"She didn't get far, so maybe her attacker didn't either," Jo said to Harry outside the hospital room. "We need everyone searching the park. It's a big area, but if we get the whole unit out searching, we might find him."

They found the knife first, in a heavily wooded area of the extensive park. As Morris had said, it was silver.

Then they found a seriously injured man up a tree. The tree had severe claw marks, and some lower branches torn off. "Well that's some of the ripping and tearing," Jo told Harry.

The unconscious man's identity was confirmed by fingerprints and DNA to be the same as the intruder at Tegan Morris' house. He also had a long history of burglary and violent offences.

When he regained consciousness, he told them he'd known Morris was a werewolf. He was a friend of her brother-in-law, who was recently arrested for killing his wife, Morris' sister. Like the brother-in-law he was a follower of prominent misogynist who had inspired the murder, a person who was now ridiculed for his claims of being imprisoned by a werewolf.

He readily admitted to attempting to break into Morris' house, and attempting to kill her, claiming that because she wasn't human it couldn't be a crime. The man was proud of his actions.

"What do we do?" Harry asked Jo back at the office.

"We have him charged with breaking and entering and attempted murder. We make sure he doesn't get bail, and we'll also ensure specially trained corrective services officers are watching him on the night of the full moon. Lucky guy. He'll always have a cell to himself."

"And the wolf?"

"She used reasonable force to defend herself. So no charges. But I will recommend she stay in our cells on the night of the full moon so she's safe from any further attackers."

Zombie

Senior Agent Jo Burns closed her front door, and clicked the button on her key to unlock her nondescript grey sedan, as she walked toward the car port. She sensed the movement before she registered what she saw. I large, muscular man walking across her front lawn, with a strange, halting, limping gait.

As he swung the knife, she reacted, grabbing the knife hand, pulling him forward off balance while she stepped aside. As he lost balance and began to fall, she kneed him in the stomach, to wind him.

While her attacker was extremely strong, he was slow and clumsy. Jo, on the other hand, was a well-trained fighter, fit and agile.

In moments her attacker was face-down on the ground, with hands cuffed behind his back. She asked his name, and he just grunted. She turned him over, face upward, and asked again. As he made further noises, she realised he had no tongue.

She'd heard of this, but never actually seen it.

"Zombie, huh? Who is pulling your strings, I wonder."

At the HDU office, pathologist Helen Thompson reported that person in the cells was Andrew Harrison, recently officially deceased, and even more recently buried. He was not dead, but under the influence of strong drugs which slowed all of his bodily functions so much he appeared dead.

Agent Marissa Tyler looked over Helen's report. "Zombie, so he wasn't acting of his own volition. Whoever did this to him wanted to kill you, Jo."

"And they probably still do. So who would want me dead?" Jo asked.

"Everyone you ever arrested as a cop. Everyone you ever arrested here. Families of monsters you've killed. You're a popular person."

"That doesn't help a lot. Although not many of them would have the knowledge or skill to create a zombie. We need a way to narrow it down. Maybe if Helen can find a way to reverse the effect of the drugs, Mr Harrison can give us some answers."

In the lab, Helen had realised Harrison was going to go through severe pain as he withdrew from the drugs. She could not provide any pain relief because any drugs she could use would lower his heart rate and respiration further, killing him. He was handcuffed to a hospital bed, sweating, and screaming, as the drugs worked their way out of his system.

For three days, the agents worked through old case files trying to find someone likely to have the ability to create a zombie, while Helen tried to keep her patient alive.

Eventually, Harrison was in a state to write his story for them. He had been hired to do garden work. The next thing he knew he was being dug up from the ground, and being ordered to attack a woman he didn't know.

He was able to identify the house where he had worked, and the woman who lived there and drugged him and gave him the order. It was the wife of a serial killer Jo had arrested years before, who was still in jail.

"What do we arrest her for?" Trainee Agent Harry Smythe asked. "Conspiracy to commit murder?"

"We don't need a charge. She won't be going through the regular system," Jo answered.

"Someone who can make anyone around them do anything, is too dangerous to go to a regular jail," Marissa explained. "She's going to have to spend the rest of her life isolated in a high-security mental health institution where she can't get access to people to influence, or to spell ingredients.

She may even need to be gagged or kept sedated for the rest of her life, for the protection of everyone around her."

"We don't kill anything unless we absolutely have to," Jo answered. "We're here to protect."

The woman was admitted to a secure institution, and where she was identified only as Mrs X.

Green

Senior Agent Jo Burns received a phone call from the HDU's police contact Inspector David Webber.

"We've got a lost child for you," David said.

"When did we become responsible for lost children?" Jo asked.

"When the kid's green."

"Green?"

"Green. Green skin. Green hair. Green eyes. Speaks, but not English, and not any language anyone here recognises. Pretty sure it's one of yours."

"I'll be right up."

She called Agent Marissa Tyler. "I'm going upstairs. Can you look something up for me? It's not in our records. It's a story or folk tale or something, from about the tenth or eleventh century about green children in England. I remember reading about it, but can't recall the details."

"Green children?"

"I think there were two in the story, but there's one upstairs. I'm going to get it."

Marissa looked at Trainee Agent Harry Smythe. "Have you ever heard of green children?" she asked. He shook his head.

In David's office, Jo found a small girl, about five years old, naked, with a blanket draped over her shoulders. David explained a driver had brought the girl into the police station after almost hitting her on the road past a National Park.

The girl seemed puzzled, but not afraid, by her surroundings and the people she didn't know. Jo took her in the lift back down to the HDU office.

Marissa had found a Wikipedia article about the two green children who had appeared in Woolpit, Suffolk in England in the early to middle eleven hundreds. She'd followed the links for the references back to the sources, to find many confused and conflicting versions of the story. Some versions of the story mentioned of a tunnel to a possibly underground place inhabited by green people. The Woolpit children had refused to eat anything except broad beans.

Jo called the HDU pathologist Helen Thompson to check the child's health, and sent both Harry and Marissa out; Harry to buy food and Marissa to get some basic child's clothes.

The little girl allowed herself to be inspected, and made some distressed noises when Helen took a blood sample, but was otherwise quiet and compliant.

When Marissa returned, the women dressed the child, who seemed confused by the process.

Harry had been unable to find broad beans. He came back with fresh green beans, and canned five bean mix. Both were put in a plate and the girl was offered a fork. She looked suspiciously at the food, then carefully picked up a soft canned bean with her fingers and delicately put it in her mouth. After chewing thoughtfully for a moment, she grabbed the canned beans by the handful and ate hungrily.

"So how do we get her back where she belongs?" Marissa asked. "I mean, she doesn't seem to be dangerous, she's not really our problem, except to get her back to her family."

"I guess we go to the area she was found, and look for an entrance to another world," Jo said. "Hopefully, our visitor will recognise something and help us find what we're looking for."

They decided to begin the search by following set bushwalking paths through the national park, thinking those would have been easier for the child to have walked along. Starting from the road, they selected the nearest walking path and began walking into the bush.

After an hour or so of walking, they could hear the roar of a waterfall nearby. The child began to act excitedly, and started to run from the path through the trees towards the sound. The three HDU agents followed.

The waterfall went over a small cliff face. Vines grew over the rocks, but something, possibly recent storms, had moved some of the vines aside, revealing a tunnel.

Following the child, all three agents sloshed their way across the furious turmoil of water at the base of the waterfall, getting soaked on the way. Inside the tunnel, they turned on the torches of their mobile phones to see, while the child simply ran on ahead unimpeded by the darkness.

The tunnel ended at a large open cave. The light from their phones would not penetrate the depths of the cave, but there were phosphorescent drawings on the walls. "They look like Aboriginal cave paintings," Jo said.

"Except for the part where they glow in the dark," Marissa responded.

"Except for that," Jo agreed.

They'd almost lost sight of the child who continued running on into the dark. In the shadows, they saw two adult figures appear, and heard the child squeal with joy as she was picked up by the taller one.

The three agents and the family stood silently looking at each other across the gloom, then the family turned and left, going further into the dark.

Exiting the tunnel, the agents moved the vines and other plants to better hide the tunnel entrance.

Yowie

Trainee Agent Harry Smythe arrived into the office early, and was shocked to discover a large ape-like creature mopping the office floor. He stood frozen to the spot, staring at the creature, not knowing what he should do.

Agent Marissa Tyler arrived. "Still working?" she said to the creature. "Running late today huh?"

The creature shrugged its shoulders, and looked past her to Harry.

"Oh, you two haven't met yet? Yowie, meet Harry, he's new here. Harry, meet the Bundamba Yowie."

The Yowie nodded to Harry and resumed his work.

"He's really a Yowie?" Harry asked.

"He's really a Yowie. We call him Yowie, which isn't really a name, but he's got used to it. He used to live in the area where the TAFE college is in Ipswich. It was a big, open area. He got his water from Bundamba Creek. It was a nice life. Humans moved into the area, and he stole chickens for food along with the native plants and animals he'd always eaten. The city of Ipswich built up all around him, but he still his his bit of open space, until the early two thousands, when the TAFE college was built in the middle of his territory."

"Wait, he was in Ipswich before they built it up. It's not a new city. How old is he?"

"No-one knows. Anyway, he went a bit aggro when people took over his home. He kept wrecking the building work overnight. It was a big deal at the time. The Education Department were freaking out their property being constantly destroyed and their cost overruns. Then Kurt Davidson got involved. I've told you about Kurt before. He was Senior Agent here at the time. He stayed on the building site overnight, and met Yowie. They talked. Well Kurt talked. Yowie used

28

gestures. Kurt went back every night until they reached an agreement. It took about a month, but Kurt didn't want to use force unless he absolutely had to. Yowie lives in one of the units in the floor below our cells. He works as an after hours cleaner for us, and the HDU provides all his meals and everything he needs, so he doesn't need a territory and doesn't run afoul of humans who don't understand."

"That floor below the cells are living units? I thought it was files or evidence of something."

"Well, the residents are kind of evidence, but files and evidence storage are the next storey down."

"And he just lives down there and never leaves?"

"Sometimes one of us will take him out to a national park or a big park late at night so he can have the night out. He's nocturnal. He enjoys a good run, and having a bit of a hunt and gather even though he doesn't need the food."

"Who else lives down there?"

"Well you remember that zombie? The one Helen looked after and finally healed? Andrew Harrison? Yeah, he didn't want to horrify his family by going home after he was officially dead and they buried him. He was a nurse before all of that, not sure how he went from nursing to the gardening job that got him into trouble. He's starting next week as Helen's assistant. He's living there. I don't think there's anyone else at the moment. Jo and I have both stayed in spare units overnight when we've had big cases on or something was happening and we couldn't go home."

Yowie was packing up his mop and bucket. He patted Harry on the head, and nodded to Marissa, then went to the lift and selected the "down" button.

Rose

A card arrived at the HDU addressed personally to Senior Agent Jo Burns.

The front of the card was black, with a red rose drawn in glitter. On the back was the message: "The Order of the Rose requests your attendance." An address, and a time that night followed the message.

Jo asked Agent Marissa Tyler to find out what the Order of the Rose was.

An hour later, Marissa reported the HDU and its sister agencies around the world had no record of an Order of the Rose. An online search, however, had produced ten Orders of the Rose, all of which were related to role playing games.

"Add to that, their card looks like some kid's arts and craft project, so it's probably nonsense we can afford to ignore," Marissa said.

"Probably," Jo replied, "and yet, they know we exist, they know my name, and they know how to get a message to us."

Jo went to the meeting, in a disused sandstone church. She knocked on the door, and it opened, so she walked in.

Inside, a dozen people in deep red cloaks, their heads and faces covered, were standing around a table with a large brass or gold cross on it. The cross was inlaid with red enamel. Beside the cross, was a brass, or gold, rose which was heavily decorated with red and green gemstones. Whether the stones were real or fakes, she couldn't tell.

One of the cloaked people spoke: "Vampire killer Jo Burns, we welcome you, and invite you to join our order." The voice was young and male.

"Um, thanks for the invitation, but I'd rather start with information. What is your order?"

"We are an ancient order, dedicated to the removal of vampires from the face of the Earth. We were founded nine hundred years ago, by a group from within the Knights Templar, who knew the danger of vampires."

Of course it was the Templars. She realised now, that the cross was a Templar cross. She had a strong suspicion they were role playing gamers who had taken things too far by getting the real authority involved.

"And these Knights Templar decided to use glitter as a logo?"

"The glitter's a modern innovation. It's a near approximation of the Rose of Jerusalem, a copy of which you see on our altar. The original is at our home in Palestine."

"Why do you want me to join your order?"

"You are known as a proficient vampire killer. We want you to join us as we hunt a vampire who has a very high profile."

He named a state politician, one Jo knew well, who was instrumental in organising supplying contaminated or out of date blood from the blood bank to vampires.

"Well, I'm not joining your club. I don't need to be part of your club to hunt vampires when it's necessary. Has anyone else in this room even faced a real-life vampire?"

There was an uncomfortable silence and an amount of fidgeting and foot shuffling.

She continued: "As I thought. Let me explain how it works here. If vampires obey the law and don't harm anyone, they're left alone. If they break the law, and become a danger to humans, my team deals with them. There's no room in this for vigilante groups to get involved. If you attack someone just because they're a vampire, my team and I will deal with you. You will either be prosecuted to the fullest extent of the law, or if you carry on about vampires and act insane, we will have you locked in a mental health facility for the rest of your life. Do you understand me?"

Silence.

"I said: 'Do you understand me?' I want an answer."

"We understand you, but we are bound by our oath to fight the evil of vampires, and we will abide by our oath even if we become martyrs to our cause."

"I don't deal with good and evil. I deal with the law. If you break the law, I will deal with you. Bear that in mind."

Jo left, and ordered round-the-clock observation of the politician they had named, in case the Order of the Rose really was stupid enough to attack him. She also called the politician and warned him of the threat.

It was two pm the next day when Jo and Trainee Agent Harry Smythe, in a car across the road from the politician's house, saw three men in dark-coloured clothes arrive and try to break in via a window. The burglar alarm blared, as the two HDU agents called for back-up and ran across the road.

None of the young men had any actual skills in fighting, and they did not resist arrest for very long.

Jo noticed all three had matching tattoos on their wrists: a Templar cross on the left wrist, and a rose on the right.

Jo recognised the voice as one of them, a young man who gave his name as John, spoke, "The others all abandoned their oath after you spoke to us."

"Well they were the smart ones. You realise the man you were hunting could have killed you far more easily than we arrested you. It might be time to give up on your game before someone gets hurt."

"We haven't gone to the home chapter for our training yet. That's why we're not very good at this. But this isn't a game. It's real. It's all over the world. We have wealthy, powerful backers. Who do you think bought the church for us?"

Who indeed? Jo was not sure what to think about any of it.

She handed the prisoners over to the police to be charged with the attempted break and enter. They wouldn't get much time for it, because it was an amateurish attempt and they'd had no chance at succeeding.

Then she wrote up her report, and circulated it to the HDU's sister agencies around the world, in case the Order of the Rose wasn't just a game.

Haunted

Gavin Burn's hand shook as he picked up his coffee cup to drink.

"What did you want to talk about?" his cousin, Senior Agent Jo Burns of the Human Defence Unit, asked.

"When I said I was going to become a paranormal investigator, you were the only one who didn't laugh at me," he said. "Everyone else treated it as a joke, but you treated it seriously. You told me to be careful, that what I was getting into was dangerous."

Jo nodded.

"Well now I'm in trouble. Something bad has happened. I was investigating this house, and I tell you it was haunted. I couldn't get rid of it. It was something more evil than I've ever faced before. I admit it, I ran. I abandoned the investigation and the people who owned the house, but the entity, whatever it was, stayed with me. Instead of the house I was investigating being haunted, now I'm being haunted. It keeps telling me things, horrible things. It wants me to kill people. It keeps showing me blood, and dismembered bodies. Please don't laugh at me. I don't know what to do. I don't know who to turn to."

Jo listened intently, then asked: "Do you know what I do for a living?"

"Sure. You're a cop. I'm not asking you to arrest a spirit, I just need someone to talk to, someone who can help me work out what to do next."

"I used to be a cop," Jo said. Then she explained her work. He looked shocked.

"Why doesn't the family know?" he asked quietly.

"My unit doesn't exist. Neither do I. Officially, I'm still just a cop. Now, I'm going to ask you to come with me to my non-existent office."

At the HDU offices, Gavin agreed to be put in a cell, so the voice could not persuade him to harm anyone.

Trainee agent Harry Smythe asked Jo, "So are we helping this ghost to finish its unresolved issues?"

"What Gavin described to me wasn't a ghost," Jo answered.

"Then what?"

"It's another kind of spirit, oppressing him. Oppression is a precursor to possession. "

"So we get an exorcist? Or what?"

"We get an exorcist. Believe it or not, we have clergy for several religions on call. Gavin doesn't practice any religion, but aligns more with Christianity than anything else, so I'm calling in a Christian minister. She'll be here soon."

Gavin stayed in the cell, while the minister, Jo, and Harry stood outside.

The minister began prayers and Bible readings, while Gavin complained about his head hurting and the spirit yelling inside his skull.

It went on for hours, with Gavin yelling and cursing, threatening and crying, screeching in languages he'd never known.

Eventually, there was a sudden lull, a sense of peace. Gavin was able to confirm he'd felt the spirit leaving.

He slept for several hours before he was ready to go home.

"Are you going to quit paranormal investigation, now you know how dangerous it is?" Jo asked.

"No. I know how dangerous it is, but now I know how important it is as well. I'm going to learn more about what I'm doing, and I'm going to find skilled people to work with instead of doing it on my own."

"Fair enough," Jo said. "When you get into trouble again, you know how to find me."

Big Bad Wolf

HDU Senior Agent Jo Burns was asleep. In her dream, she was following a little girl in a red hooded cloak through a strange purple forest.

"Slow down!" she called to the girl.

The girl replied, in her deceased daughter Katie's voice, "Hurry Mummy! Watch out for the big bad wolf. Don't let him catch you!"

Jo looked up to see the full moon, and heard the long howl.

She woke up with a start, to see a long-nosed hairy face, with eyes reflecting purple in the low light, close in to her own face.

"What big eyes you have, Grandma," Jo said, as she raised both feet and used them to push the wolf away. She scrambled out of the tangled sheets and blanket and ran from the room.

The wolf picked itself up and followed.

"Run Mummy!" she heard her daughter's voice from her dream. "The big bad wolf is coming."

She could hear the wolf gaining as she ran into her home study, and locked the door behind her. It was a heavy, solid door, but it wouldn't hold the wolf for long. Just long enough, Jo hoped.

She opened a cupboard door, to reveal her gun safe, and entered the code.

The door to the room splintered as the gun safe opened.

Adrenaline pumping, Jo grabbed her service weapon, and a sliver bullet from the box.

She tried to load the gun, her hands shaking. The wolf entered the room. It was almost on top of her, when she heard Katie's voice yelling, "No! Go away big bad wolf!"

The wolf flew backwards hitting the wall high up, and sliding down.

Jo loaded the gun.

As the wolf got up again, she fired.

The wolf collapsed, bleeding, panted rapidly for a few moments, whimpered and died.

"Katie?" Jo called hesitantly to the room.

There was no answer.

"Katie? Are you here?"

The dark empty room did not answer.

"Katie!" Jo yelled to the darkness.

Still, the darkness failed to answer.

Katie was dead. She was a small child. What unfinished business could she have, strong enough to keep her in the living world? There had to be another explanation for what had just happened.

Ghoul

Pathologist Helen Thompson called HDU Senior Agent Jo Burns. She said, "Come down to the lab, and see what's on the slab."

Jo asked, "Did you just rewatch Rocky Horror?"

"Yes, but I'm serious. You're going to have to see what I've got on the slab to believe it," she said.

When Jo arrived, she was greeted with the smell of decomposition, and saw a strange creature. It was a human-shaped thing, with green skin, numerous stitched lacerations, a flat-topped bald head, with strange bolt-like projections from the sides of the head.

"This was a person?" Jo asked.

"Multiple people," Helen answered. "The green colour of the skin is dye, it's mottled because of decomposition."

"So someone tried to recreate Frankenstein's monster? And those projections from the side of the head?"

"Shaped from ear tissue as far as I can tell."

"Was it alive?"

"The individuals used to be, but the agglomeration, no."

"That's some consolation. Where was the body found?"

"Frederick Street, Toowong."

"Near the cemetery?"

"Yes. You know who did this?"

"I've got a theory."

"Tell me."

"It's a ghoul, playing with its food."

"Now I wish you hadn't told me. Do you want me to run DNA on the parts?"

"No need. The only use for the information would be to notify relatives, and they don't need to know this. Cremate it. Put the ashes somewhere nice."

Toowong Cemetery was a huge area for the HDU agents to search.

Jo ordered them to spread out, and look for any signs of ghoul activity. She'd issued all agents net launchers. When the trigger was pulled the net would launch and, if aimed properly, would trap whatever they were fired at.

It was late afternoon, moving into evening, the sun starting to go down. This was when ghouls began their day, moving out from their hiding places, searching for the grave they would rob for the night's meal.

Agents checked in over the radio from different parts of the cemetery: "No sightings." Over and over again: "No sightings."

Jo began to despair of finding their quarry, when Trainee Agent Harry Smythe's excited voice announced: "Hey, there's a dingo here. I didn't know we had dingoes in Brisbane!"

"Net it!" Jo commanded, running toward his location.

Harry shot the dingo with a net as it ran away. He approached, and pulled the ropes of the net together to prevent the dingo from escaping.

Jo pulled a sandwich out of a pack she'd been carrying on her back.

"A sandwich?" Harry asked.

"Normal food." Jo answered. "Makes them return to their real shape. Help me force it to eat."

Through the net they pulled the dingo's mouth opened, forced the sandwich in, and then held the mouth closed.

"My father used to rub the dog's nose to make it swallow its pills," Jo said. "Let's see if this works."

While Harry held the mouth closed, Jo rubbed the nose.

The dingo convulsed, stretched and contracted, and eventually there was a creature, shaped like an emaciated human man, with grey skin, lying in the net.

"Wow," Harry said. "So we're arresting it?"

"Nope," Jo answered. "Ghouls aren't like the other creatures we hunt. There's nothing human about them. They're miserable, starving, demons, forced into our dimension, and condemned to feed on the dead. There's only one thing to do with them. Stand back."

Jo kept a boot on the ghoul, holding it on the ground, while Harry moved back as commanded.

Jo pulled out her standard service weapon, an ordinary gun with ordinary bullets.

"Once they've eaten normal food, they're projection into this reality is weak," she said.

She squeezed the trigger.

The grey head exploded, and then the ghoul's whole body vanished.

"It's dead?" Harry asked. "Or is it just back wherever demons come from?"

"Hopefully both," Jo answered.

Save Daddy

HDU Senior Agent Jo Burns was running down the labyrinthine corridors, with unnamed doors, of the HDU, chasing a little girl who was wearing a red hooded cloak.

As the girl disappeared around the corner at the end of the corridor, her deceased daughter's voice came to her: "Hurry, Mummy, we have to save Daddy."

Jo woke up with a start, echoing from her dream, she heard Katie's voice say a word Katie had been far too young to know: "Vampire."

Jo tried to phone David, but got no answer. She dressed quickly and took a small concealable crossbow and three wooden bolts from her gun safe. She knew if she missed with the first bolt there was probably not much chance she would be able to reload, but she habitually took extra.

At David's house, she didn't get an answer when she knocked at the door. She heard David yell from inside. They had each other's spare keys for emergencies. Jo determined this to be an emergency and let herself in. She heard a crash from the back of the house, David's study, and ran there.

Through the open doorway, she could see a female vampire had David pinned against the wall, and was about to bite him.

"I'm late to the party, again," Jo said.

Startled, the vampire turned partly towards Jo.

It was enough to create the space where Jo could fire without harming David. She pulled the trigger mechanism, releasing the wooden bolt. The force from the crossbow staked the vampire and she fell to the floor.

David, shaking, slowly bent his knees and sat down on the floor, leaning against the wall.

"Are you OK? Did she bite you?" Jo asked.

David put his hands over his face. "She didn't bite me. Is she dead?"

Jo sat on the floor beside David. "She's kind of dead. They can be brought back, and there are people crazy enough to do it. The clean up team will cut her head off, fill every orifice with garlic, cremate the head and body separately, and scatter both lots of ashes in different locations. The idea is to make sure no-one can gather the bits back together. You invited her in."

"First time I've been on a date, since... It seemed to be going well. I invited her back here for a drink."

"Do me a favour, don't invite people into your house unless you know them really well. I might be too late next time."

"How did you know to come this time? You weren't just passing by my study."

"Katie told me, in a dream."

"Katie?"

"Yeah. It's the second time she's given me a warning. Saved me from a werewolf."

"Our dead daughter told my ex-wife to save me from a vampire. That's a sentence I never expected to ever say."

"Life got weird."

"Did I say 'thank you'?"

"It was implied." Jo noticed what had smashed. "Your grandmother's sculpture."

"Yeah, well, she wasn't much of a sculptor." He paused a thoughtful moment and asked: "Why didn't we make it? After Katie, I mean."

"We both needed each other, but we were each so caught up in our own grief, neither of us had anything left for the other."

"And Katie's back now?"

"Katie, or something impersonating her. If it's Katie, it means she has unfinished business."

"Could that be us?"

"Could be."

They sat, side by side, each lost in their own thoughts.

Gingerbread

HDU Senior Agent Jo Burns was sitting across the desk from Inspector David Webber in his office.

"I don't know," he said. "This could be one of yours, or it could be a run of the mill psychopath. I think I need you onboard, just in case."

"What's the case?" Jo asked.

"The Gap's a relatively affluent suburb, not much crime, except for white collar."

Jo nodded.

"It's usually considered safe enough that kids can walk or ride their bikes to school. But yesterday, two children didn't get home. The day before, a girl told her parents a strange woman in black with a funny hat had tried to grab her, but she'd kicked the woman up the shins and ran away."

"Quick thinking."

"This morning, another kid left home for school and didn't make it there."

"So we have three missing kids?"

Jo took a deep breath and let it out slowly. She and David both knew first-hand the horror of a child going missing.

"So your people are going door to door in the area?" Jo asked.

"Yes. So far no-one's claimed to have seen anything, but we're door knocking anyway. Will you get your team involved?"

"Of course. I don't know what we're looking for, but we'll go search the area. I presume you've got the routes the children normally travelled to and from school."

David handed her the file. "This is your copy. You know everything we know."

"Thanks. I'll grab my agents and head out now."

"What exactly are we looking for?" Trainee Agent Harry Smythe asked.

"Anything that doesn't belong or doesn't seem to fit in," Jo answered. All three kids' routes to school meet up at this point, so they were probably taken somewhere between here and the school. From here they turned from Waterworks Road to Settlement Road, and then it's only a block or so to the school. Somewhere in these last couple of minutes of walking, they disappeared. So while the police are going door to door, and our other agents are searching the wider area, the three of us are walking where these kids walked, and seeing what they saw."

Jo, Harry and Agent Marissa Tyler walked in silence. There was an independent supermarket on one corner of the intersection, a park and ride carpark beside the bus stop on another, a house on another, and the fourth had the corner of the school grounds. From this turn, they were walking on Settlement Road, on the opposite side of the road from the school. Before reaching the pedestrian crossing across the busy road, there was a smaller, three-way, intersection, where Bromwich Street ended at Settlement road.

Between Bromwich Street and the pedestrian crossing was an empty yard. "I think the house that used to be here burned down a year or so ago," Marissa said. "Looks like the owners have decided not to rebuild." She pointed to a real estate agent's sign.

"Is this what it looks like?" Harry asked.

"It looks like an empty yard with a for 'sale sign'," Marissa said.

"Can't you see it? It's right there!" Harry seemed confused.

"What can you see?" Jo asked.

"You can't see it either?" Harry answered.

Out of nowhere, sounding as if it was coming from a long distance away, Jo heard the voice of her deceased daughter: "Handsel and Gretel found a gingerbread house."

Suddenly she could see it. "It's a gingerbread house," she said.

"It's a what?" Marissa asked.

"Harry saw it because he's younger than us. He's closer to being a kid. I can see it now, because Katie helped me."

"Katie helped you?" Marissa sounded worried.

"I'll explain to you later." Jo continued. "Here's what you can't see: It's a gingerbread house. There's jelly beans on the stair risers. The door is red and white striped like a candy cane, and there's candy canes along the back fence. The flowers in front are lollypops, and the leaves are spearmint leaves lollies There's a tree which seems to be a liquorice strap, with more spearmint leaves. Curtains in the windows look like red and white gingham, but I think it's more of the same type of lolly as the candy canes. There's other lollies and white icing decorations. The front stairs and the edges around the door and windows are chocolate. The roof seems to be drizzled white icing." Jo walked around the strange house. "There's no other walls," she continued." It's a single house-sized gingerbread biscuit. It's a gingerbread house, directly across the road from the school."

Harry picked up a lolly from the lawn.

"Don't eat that. Don't eat anything," Jo instructed. "Harry, you're with me. Marissa, call David for backup. Tell him to get any young constables, anyone under thirty here."

With Harry beside her, Jo knocked on the hard, but slightly sticky front door.

As the door started to open inwards, Jo forced her way in.

47

An old woman in a long black dress and pointy black hat was pushed inside as the door was forced.

They were inside a single large room, with a bench and a pot or cauldron hanging over a fire in an old-fashioned fire place, fire pokers and other implements on a rack beside the fire, cooking implements on a bench nearby and a large wooden table with one wooden chair.

Jo said, "Good morning madam, we're looking for some missing children. Have you seen any smallish people around here?"

"You can't just push your way in here!" the old woman yelled. "Do you have a warrant?"

"I don't need a warrant. I'm not that kind of a cop, and you're not that kind of little old lady are you? Turn and face the wall. Put your hands up against the wall."

The witch screeched, and began to make some strange movements with her hand. Jo picked up a fireplace poker and brought it down hard on the woman's arms.

"Just in case you use hands for spells," Jo said. The woman, with injured, possibly broken, arms, was whimpering. Despite the injury, Jo handcuffed her, and pushed her up agains the wall.

"If she moves at all, shoot her," Jo told Harry. "We don't know what she's capable of."

Jo ran up the stairs, and found, on the next floor, another big open room. This one contained six cages, like giant budgerigar cages. Three of them were occupied by small children. A large key was hanging on a nail on the wall. Jo used it to release the kids. She was about to lead them down the stairs when she heard a yell and a shot.

"Wait here," Jo instructed the kids.

Downstairs she found the witch bleeding out. Harry was holding a gun, looking pale. Behind him were three young

48

police officers, one of whom now seemed to be turned to stone, or at least a gigantic boiled lolly.

"Harry, give me the gun," she said.

Harry, shaking, handed it to her.

She pointed to the transformed cop. "Take her outside. I think the magic only works in here." She hoped the magic only worked inside the house. Two constables carried their colleague outside. Jo looked around, found a table cloth and threw it over the witch's corpse.

She went back and had the children follow her down the stairs. There, she took the shaken Harry by the arm, and led everyone outside.

In the yard, was a sugar statue.

David was there already, and Jo handed the children over to him.

"Katie helped again?" he asked quietly.

"Marissa told you?"

"Yeah. This is getting weird."

"Tell me about it."

She looked back at the gingerbread house, and saw it was fading, and its sugar decorations melting. As it faded out of existence, the police officer who had been transformed slowly seemed to fade back into humanity.

"What just happened?" Harry asked.

"You killed the wicked witch. Her spells must be dying with her," Jo said.

Countess

HDU Trainee Agent Harry Smythe woke from what seemed an incredibly deep sleep. As his eyes struggled to focus, his brain registered the letter A, nothing else.

"Wha..." he struggled to say.

"You're safe now," a soft female voice said.

He drifted back to sleep again and eventually woke properly.

He was lying on an ornate antique couch, in expensively decorated room. An elegant woman with long black hair, in a floor-length red formal dress sat on an armchair. On a ribbon around her neck, she wore a black jewel, with the letter A on it in red.

"Welcome back to the world of the living. I am Countess Anastasia Arafami. You may address me as 'Your Ladyship'. You are safe now. You have not been bitten or in any way harmed, not since I brought you here. I have summoned Senior Agent Burns to collect you."

"Where am I?" he asked groggily. "I mean, where am I, Your Ladyship."

"You are in my house. I rescued you from a vampire who was about to bite you. I do not normally fight my own kind, but I, and my household, respect the truce Senior Agent Burns brokered. We buy our blood, and do not take from unwilling humans."

A younger woman, who looked very much like the Countess led Jo Burns into the room.

Jo bowed slightly to the countess, and said, "Thank you Your Ladyship. Your kindness is very much appreciated."

"I did not act out of kindness, but self-interest," the Countess replied. "One does not live five hundred years without learning which fights to avoid. You are an opponent I would rather not fight against."

"The feeling is mutual. With your permission, I will take my agent and leave."

The Countess nodded. Jo pulled Harry's arm around her shoulder and half-led half-carried him to her car. They drove back to the HDU office in silence.

Back in the office, Jo called HDU pathologist Helen Thompson to check on Harry's health. Helen brought her assistant, Andrew Harrison, a former zombie, with her.

Andrew passed a magnifying glass to Helen, who found a slight abrasion on Harry's neck. She asked for antiseptic and a clean dressing, which Andrew provided.

"There was a bite," Helen said. "It's not deep, but who knows. Traditionally it takes three bites to turn someone, but there have been cases…" Her voice trailed off. She looked at Jo. Jo looked back. What neither wanted to say was clear.

"What do you remember?" Jo asked.

"I was out at a nightclub. It's after hours. It's my own business what I do. I met this girl, I don't remember her name. We had a drink together, and then I woke up and the Countess was there."

"What the Countess told me was she interrupted a vampire about to make you dinner."

"We have to catch the woman. What if she goes after someone else?" Harry was earnest.

"No need. The Countess will have taken care of the fang involved. What we have to do, is to watch you and make sure you don't turn."

"Turn? You mean?"

"Yes. I'm afraid you're spending the night in the cells."

"Can we trust the Countess? Maybe she didn't interrupt. Maybe she was working with the girl I met."

"The Countess is one of the fangs I negotiated with to create the agreement whereby vampires get old or infected blood from the blood bank. She knows the HDU will kill any fang we find feeding off humans. She's nothing if not a pragmatist. She saved you as a strategic move in dealing with the HDU. It's an alliance that works for her. She's the oldest, most powerful fang in the area, and most of the others obey her, a number even live in her house. In fang politics, she's the equivalent of the Prime Minister, Governor-General, the Dalai Lama, and a High Court judge rolled into one. Not all fangs give their allegiance to her, but the smart ones do. We can trust her because the agreement works for her and keeps her subjects safe from us. She's the most dangerous thing we've ever dealt with, but we can trust her for now."

Harry unhappily went to a cell and was locked in for the night. In the next cell was a werewolf, in voluntarily so as to not do any harm on the full moon. The wolf cringed, and backed away from the wall the two cells shared. Jo noticed, but didn't say anything to Harry. She wanted to be certain.

In the morning, the wolf had become a woman, who told Jo she had felt frightened, and didn't know why during the night, but she would still be back next full moon.

In his cell, Harry was in a bad state. He was aggressive, yelling that he was hungry.

Jo called Helen, who came with Andrew behind her.

When Jo unlocked the cell, Harry came running out, trying to grab Helen.

Andrew grabbed Harry's arms from behind, pulled them back and held them. Andrew was no longer under the spell which had made him a zombie slave, was still extremely strong in its aftermath. He held Harry by the arms as easily as a child holds a butterfly by the wings.

Helen examined the struggling Harry.

"Sorry," she said. "He's dead. No heartbeat, skin's cold. He's a vampire."

"Get him back in the cell," Jo told Andrew. "I've got a call to make."

An hour later, the Countess arrived at the HDU headquarters. She had brought two bags of blood. She entered the cell, opened a bag, and gave it to Harry. He drank, hesitantly at first, and then hungrily. After the second bag, Harry sat on the bed in the cell and cried.

"This is hard," the Countess said, "but it will get easier. You will learn to live as a vampire. If you choose to hunt your own food, I will not stop you, unless your choices affect the stability of my people. I recommend, however, you become one of my people. Come to live in the house with other vampires, it is easier when you are one of many. We do not harm humans, now. We live among them. You are now a vampire, and you will choose how you will live as one of us. I will leave you to think."

In Jo's office, the Countess asked, "What will you do with him now? I have invited him to join my community, but I will not force him."

"Honestly, if he can control the blood thirst, and doesn't harm humans, I have no problem with releasing him, either to your care or on his own."

"It will be best if Harry were to stay in your cell for a few more days, and I will bring him food, until he has begun to come to terms with the change he has undergone."

"I'm fine with that. I'd like to give him the best chance possible."

"Will he be able to continue his work here? It will be good for him, for his mind, if he can continue some of his past life."

"Again, if he can refrain from harming people, I don't see why not. I do see that would give you a vampire in the HDU."

"And it would give you an agent in my community."

"It's lucky we have the agreement."

"Indeed it is fortunate we have the agreement. It would be difficult if we were enemies."

Creature

It was Trainee Agent Harry Smythe's first day back, or rather night, at work after extended sick leave. He was now on permanent night shift. He felt weird putting a bag of blood in the lunch room fridge, but was determined to work as normal.

The first person he saw was Andrew Harrison, assistant to the pathologist. Andrew, unable to speak since his time as a zombie, carried a notebook with him for conversations.

Andrew wrote: "Sorry I had to restrain you. I know how hard it is when your whole life is turned around like this. If you need to talk, I'm here."

Harry thanked him, and agreed that for the first time he felt he understood some of what Andrew had been through.

Senior Agent Jo Burns saw them and approached. She welcomed Harry back and told him to let her know if at any time he felt strange or thought work was too stressful.

Harry told her he was fine, and that he thought he'd found a case. He showed Jo a photo, which was mostly of fog.

"There's too much fog to see anything much. I can make out trees, and a river, and something…"

"The person who took the photo swears it's a monster like the Loch Ness monster in Scotland."

"The man who took the photos of the Loch Ness monster confessed to faking the photos."

"Well this woman says she didn't fake it. She shared it on social media. I can show you her story. She was out walking and saw this thing moving through the fog. I got in contact with her, and got the exact location."

"Is there any allegation this thing is dangerous in any way? We are the Human Defence Unit after all, not the Crytozoology Unit."

"I thought, maybe we should check it out, and find out what we can about it, in case it turns out to be dangerous."

"OK, go ahead. Take Marissa with you. You'll need to take your own lights. Check out the site of the photo. Look closely, and the location they gave you is the same as the photo. If you find any sign of something living there, contact the Turrbal community. You'll find a tribal council or similar on the internet. See if someone can give you information about any creatures they have traditional stories about. Tell them you're a grad student, and your institution will pay for their time, get information on how they want to be paid."

Andrew wrote a note: "I'm off shift. Is it OK if I go too? I haven't been outside in a while."

"Sure,.."

An hour later, Harry, Andrew and Marissa were walking along a stretch of the Brisbane River.

They found a lot of footprints, all human, clearly in Doc Martens boots.

"Either it's a hoax, or a lot of people wearing the same pair of boots have been out here looking for the creature," Marissa said. "Don't be too disappointed, we have wild goose chases every now and then."

Andrew had wandered off a bit further among the trees, following the direction of one trail of the boot prints, and was now furiously waving at them.

When Marissa looked over in that direction, she ran to him.

Harry stayed back, sitting on a large rock near the river bank.

Andrew pointed to a jumble of bits of painted tyre, boards, and other things.

"Congratulations, Andrew, you've found the mysterious Brisbane River monster," Marissa said.

They walked back and found Harry sitting with his head in his hands.

"Go away," Harry said.

"That's no way to talk to your superior," Marissa said.

"Go away! We've been here for hours. I haven't eaten, and I'm hungry."

Andrew wrote a note: "I'll stay with him. Go and get the blood."

Marissa ran to the car and drove away.

"You should have gone too," Harry said. "I don't know if I can control it."

Andrew wrote: "I'll take a chance. I trust you." A moment later, he added. "I'm already dead, anyway, at least officially. What more could you do to me?"

Harry looked at the page and laughed. Then he broke down, crying, and told Andrew how scared he was of hurting the people he cared about, how the hunger seemed to overtake him and he couldn't control it, how strange the vampire community he was living in was.

Andrew rested a hand on Harry's shoulder, and listened, nodding occasionally. He knew what it was to have life as he knew it suddenly end, and have to work out what a new life looked like afterwords.

It took Marissa an hour to get back with Harry's bag of blood. She turned away to avoid watching him drink, but Andrew stayed with him, hand on his shoulder, until he'd fed and felt better.

On the drive back to headquarters, Marissa said, "In future, Harry, you're taking an esky in the car when you go out in the field, and Andrew, if you're coming out in the field again, we're getting you a whistle so you can call out."

Full Moon

Jo Burns looked up at the full moon. It looked closer, bigger than it ever had before.

There'd been a time when she'd thought the moon beautiful, romantic, even. That seemed like a lifetime ago, before her daughter's death, before she'd discovered a world hidden from humans, before she joined the Human Defence Unit.

For three months, three full moons, there'd been deaths in the Southbank area. They'd been horrible deaths, bodies shredded by teeth and claws. There was a wolf on the prowl, and this full moon, she and her team planned to capture or kill the beast.

Some werewolves were fine.They knew what they became and they took steps to prevent themselves from endangering the people around them. Some were spending the full moon voluntarily locked up in the HDU cells.

Others didn't care what horror and chaos they caused. The HDU hunted those down, and usually killed them because options for dealing with a lycanthrope in wolf form were limited. They couldn't be reasoned with, and they were practically impossible to capture.

Tonight, amid the theatre goers around the Performing Arts Centre area and restaurant crowds in the Parklands area, Jo and her agents patrolled the entire Southbank precinct.

Jo stood on the pedestrian bridge and looked at the moon's reflection on the river. Passing boats broke up the reflection and sent bits of the reflected light rippling in all directions.

A bat flew past her. Trainee Agent Harry Smythe was trying out new skills, which he insisted would help with surveillance. He'd told Jo he couldn't see very well in bat form, but his hearing was incredible, and he would definitely hear an attack before human agents saw signs of it. Harry flew off into dark shadows under Parklands trees.

Somewhere out in the night was Andrew Harrison, who was officially dead and was working in the HDU pathology department. Because he was mute as a result of the efforts of a witchcraft practitioner to turn him to a zombie, one of the agents had given him a whistle to use to call for backup.

"Vampire, zombie, if the Yowie from the cleaning crew starts coming out on cases, we'll just need a wolf and a ghost for the full set," she said to herself. Then she remembered her dead daughter had helped her on some recent cases. They had a ghost.

Agent Marissa Tyler's voice came over the radio: "Andrew's blowing his whistle over in the shadows behind the Piazza. I'm headed there now. Jo started running.

When she arrived, she saw what she would later look back on as the strangest sight of her career. In police parlance the wolf was being "detained". In actuality it was lying flat on its stomach, with a zombie and a naked vampire lying across it pinning it down.

Marissa was attempting to wrap a cable tie-type handcuff around the wolf's muzzle while it struggled. Jo came up beside her and held the creature's mouth closed, so Marissa could tie the mouth shut. Then they went for the paws. Cuffing first both front paws together, then both back paws. For good measure they cuffed the back paws to the front.

Jo looked Harry in the eye, careful not to look anywhere else, and said, "The bat thing might be useful, but in future, you need a plan for clothes."

Harry turned red, then seemed to twist and shrink and changed back into a bat.

Marissa went for a car, pulling up and double-parking in Stanley Street. Andrew threw the wolf in the back seat.

They drove back to the Roma Street Police Station, pulled into the police parking area, then went through a normally-hidden door into the HDU carpark.

The wolf was hauled out and dumped in a cell for the night.

Next morning, Jo checked the cell and found a distressed, crying young woman.

Her story was that she was a police officer. A couple of months earlier she'd been called out to a dog attack. The dog had bitten her before getting away.

Since then, she'd had a couple of nights when she lost time, and had strange, horrible dreams.

She was horrified when Jo explained what she now was, and what she had done.

"What do I do now?" she asked.

Jo told her about the wolves who volunteered to spend the night of the full moon in the cells, and she readily agreed to do that.

"So, how do I just go back to normal police work on the streets, now that I know this other world exists?" she asked.

Jo remembered her own horrible introduction to the world of monstrous creatures, how going back to regular policing just hadn't been an option for her.

Jo made her an offer.

That was how Trainee Agent Kate Murdoch joined the HDU.

Fake

The body was lying face down, half covered in overgrown grass.

"Council workers clearing the overgrown creek area found the body. When they realised what it was they stopped work and called triple zero." Inspector David Webber said.

"What makes you think it's one of ours?" HDU Senior Agent Jo Burns asked.

With a gloved hand, David moved some of the long red hair, to show a huge gash across the woman's throat.

"There should have been a lot of blood, but there isn't any."

"So you think it's a fang."

A young woman who had accompanied Jo inhaled deeply. "Not a vampire," she said. "I only smell humans."

David looked at her. "Haven't I seen you around the station? Weren't you a uniform constable?"

"I, ah, transferred, sir."

"Sorry, I should have introduced you. Inspector David Webber, meet my new Trainee Agent, Kate Murdoch, and yes, I did poach her from your uniform branch."

"What happened to your old trainee, the gawky kid?"

"Harry's been promoted. He's a full agent now, he's full time night shift."

"Full time night shift? At his age nights should be for fun."

"I don't want him having too much fun. I'd have to arrest him if he did."

"Am I missing something?"

"He's had a bit of a transformation."

"And your new trainee being able to smell humans or vampires?"

"A special skill."

"So what do you smell?" David asked Kate.

"The victim was already dead when she was brought here. Her scent is mixed with the scent of early decay, and blood, no lingering scent of her alive. There is blood, you'll find a trace on her clothes, I can smell it, not a lot but it's definitely there. There have been lots of people here some very sweaty men, who were probably the council workers, lots of more recent scents, probably police, and older scents that came here when she came here. Those were teenaged girls."

"Teenaged girls? Are you sure?"

"Hormones in the sweat, and cheap supermarket body spray, overly sweet."

"Can you track where they came from or where they went?"

"Like a tracker dog?"

"I didn't want to put it that way, but yes, like that."

"I think so."

Kate led the way, through the uncut long shoulder-height grass.

"We'll struggle to find evidence in this," David said. More quietly, he asked Jo, "Werewolf?"

Jo nodded.

"Her nose is always this good?"

"Close to the full moon it is. If this case had come up near the new moon, she doesn't do anywhere near as well."

"My hearing is remarkably good near the full moon as well," Kate said.

"Sorry," Jo said.

"And your old trainee?" David asked, no longer bothering to whisper.

"Fang."

"Since when?"

"Since he had a bit too much to drink on a night out. Luckily the Countess rescued him.

"Do you trust the Countess?"

"I trust her to act in her own interests." To Kate, Jo said: "Is this the way they came or the way they went after dumping the body?"

"Both. They took almost the same path both ways I'm following the blood, so the path they took to get there. They returned walking parallel to us, but about a meter to our right. I'm not walking exactly on top of the path the path they took to avoid interfering with forensics, or scents if, you know, you decide to get a dog to do this."

They walked in silence a bit further, struggling against the long, tangled, half-dry grass.

"Just up ahead, lots of blood, probably the murder scene," Kate said.

They approached carefully, aware of the risk of trampling evidence. Grass had been trampled, and there was a significant amount of blood on the ground and grass.

"That certainly seems to be the missing blood," Jo said. "So definitely one for the regular police. All yours, David."

"That's not all the blood. I can smell some further on and I can hear girl's voices." Kate pointed on further ahead.

"Maybe we could continue the interagency cooperation a little longer?" David asked.

"Sure," Jo answered. "Please lead the way, Kate."

Another ten metres through the grass, and then they were at the back fence of a yard which backed on to the creek area.

"The cubby house, between the fence and the house," Kate said. "One said, 'We have to drink it if we want to be real vampires.' The other said, 'I'm not so sure of this now.' The first said, 'You were sure when we killed her.' The second said, 'It didn't seem real then, but this is real, and it's blood. It's her blood.'"

Jo said to David. "Well, that gives you everything you need for an arrest. You don't need us to apprehend two little girls playing vampire. If we're not involved you can go through proper channels, courts, and suchlike more easily."

David agreed it was definitely a matter for the police. He phoned for officers to come to make the arrest. Jo and Kate turned to walk back the way they'd come.

"Oh Kate," he said, "if you ever want to come back to the police force, I can make sure your old job is open."

"No thanks, sir," she said. "Now I know what's out there, I don't want to spend my time chasing delusional teens."

"Fair enough." David answered.

Bunyip

The HDU team were dressed in orange hi vis rescue uniforms. It wasn't normal attire for a secret organisation, but it would fit in with all the other searchers who had set out from the lavender farm.

Senior Agent Jo Burns briefed them. "We're parked here, because this is as far as vehicles can go. The creature grabbed the child here, and dragged her across the lavender field. It's easy to follow the path here, because of the damage to the lavender plants, but once the track gets to the forest, that's where everyone's lost it. Search and rescue brought in sniffer dogs, but they've just gone nuts. Maybe it's all the mangled lavender plants, maybe it's something else. Harry can't search from the air until dark, but he will join us then, if we haven't already found the child. Any questions."

Agent Marissa Tyler had a question. "What is the creature?"

"The girl's parents said it had the body of a seal and the face of an owl."

"A chimera?"

"Could be, but it's also one of the known descriptions of a bunyip. There's endless descriptions of bunyips and they're all contradictory, so your guess is as good as mine," Jo said. "Right, so to start we just follow the trail of floral destruction."

As they walked, Trainee Agent Kate Murdoch said, "I know why the dogs went nuts. I'm struggling here with the scents. I can smell lots of lavender, the child, and then this overbearing, overpowering, frightening scent of something I can't place. It's not like anything I've ever smelled before and it's making me feel sick."

"Can you stick with it?" Jo asked.

"Yes, it's horrible, but I'll deal with it. I should be able to cope."

They walked across the field following the path of destruction.

"How big would something have to be to leave drag marks like this?" Marissa asked.

"Big," Jo answered. "The parents said the drag marks were the thing dragging its body. It actually threw the kid on its back. Kid was just too terrified to move."

Arriving at the edge of the lavender plants, they could see massive damage to the plants in the rainforest where previous searchers had already gone.

"Not that way," Kate said. "It had already made that path when it came, and it looks worse because so many people have trampled it. You see there are lots of other well-worn paths through the forest? It uses them regularly. I can smell traces some older, some new. The most recent is this way."

She led them over what looked like a bushwalking track. "I think it only churned up the soil in the lavender farm so much because that soil was already broken up for growing the plants. In here, the soil's better held together, and it's got its regular tracks. They could be bushwalking tracks or wallaby tracks, no-one seeing them would question it."

Kate led them along the path through the forest, to a creek. Playing in the shallow water, was a five year old girl, splashing around with a creature the size Labrador, that looked like a seal with an owl's face.

"What the hell?" Marissa said.

"That fits the description the parents gave of the creature, but it's so much smaller," Jo said.

They approached slowly. "Hey, Jamie, you're Jamie, right?" Jo said.

The little girl looked up. "Hello," she said.

"Your Mum and Dad are looking for you," Jo said. "We've come to take you home."

"I'm playing with my friend," the girl said.

"And it looks like you're both having lots of fun," Jo said, "but it's time to go home now. Say good-bye to your friend, and we'll go back to your home now."

The girl hugged the strange animal. "Bye bye friend," she said. "Play again tomorrow?"

"Ah, Boss," Marissa said. "Turn around very slowly."

Jo did as instructed. A massive creature which looked like a super-sized version of the animal the girl was playing with was there. She was between a very dangerous-looking animal and its young.

Marissa raised her gun, which had been loaded with animal tranquilliser darts.

"Friend's Mummy," the little girl said, and ran to the larger creature, throwing her arms around a front flipper."

"Don't shoot," Jo ordered. "Everyone stay calm." If only she could obey her own instructions. She moved very slowly towards the mother.

It looked at her with steely eyes. That beak looked as if it could tear a human apart.

"Got to go home now, Friend's Mother," the girl said. "Bye bye."

The child walked over to Jo and took her hand. The creature seemed to nod at Jo.

Jo slowly walked away, leading the child to the path. Her team slowly, quietly followed, Marissa taking the rear position, walking backward with the gun raised.

"What are we going to do about it?" Marissa whispered.

"Do about it?" Jo answered, quietly.

"The bunyip or whatever?"

"How about we leave it alone?" Jo said. "Apart from being lousy at arranging play dates, it doesn't seem to have done anything wrong. And for all we know they could be close to extinction."

"Didn't the stories of bunyips say they were dangerous? Is it safe to just let it be so close to humans?" Kate asked.

"Yes they did," Jo said. "Stories also say werewolves, vampires, zombies and Yowies are dangerous, but we know it depends on the individual. I'm not killing something that hasn't harmed anyone."

Kate blushed.

Jo continued, "I will try to swing some funding to fence the forest off from the local farms."

There was a loud screeching sound from the forest behind them.

"Let's make that electrified fencing," Jo added.

They returned the wet, dirty, tired and happy child to her parents, who would tell them her own story, whether the parents believed it or not. The HDU agents simply said they'd found her playing in the shallow creek.

The Red

It was Agent Harry Smythe's night off. Night off, because just as he could no longer work days, he could no longer do anything else during the day.

He'd not known what to do with a night off. In fact he'd actually asked the Countess Anastasia Arafami, what to do.

The Countess, who owned the house where he and many other vampires lived, looked at him strangely. "Harry," she said. "You know my rules, and your boss's rules. Don't feed on a human. Apart from that you are free to do whatever you like. What did you do on nights off when you were human?"

Harry thought about it. He used to go out clubbing. He could still do that. He could enjoy music. He might even find someone who wanted to dance with him, or more. Was he ready for a possible relationship? Not when he was living in the Countess' house, afraid of what he might do.

As a precaution, he drank a pack of 0+, supplied by the blood bank, so that he would not get hungry while out.

The club was exactly as he remembered it, except, with heightened senses, the music was louder, sweaty humans were smellier, the beer he could no longer drink smelled more of hops and malt, and people talked louder to be heard over the general wall of sound. Disappointingly, human heartbeats did not keep time with the music.

Harry decided the club was overwhelming. He'd just go for a walk, or perhaps a fly.

As he was leaving, someone bumped into him. The man stepped back and Harry realised simultaneously that he was a vampire, and that he'd pressed something the size of a business card into his hand.

Outside, Harry looked at the card. It was black, with a stylised picture of vampire fangs dripping blood. There were no words on the card.

Harry re-entered the club, but could not find the vampire.

He returned to the Countess' house, showed her the card and asked if she knew what it meant.

She looked at the card, went paler than her usual milk-white, and said. "They're here. I've run all across the world and they're here." To Harry, she said, "This is the card of an organisation called The Red. They are vampires who believe we are a superior race, and that feeding on humans is our right. In my own home country I had established a community like this one here, where vampires could live in peace with humans, by only consuming blood harvested by blood banks, which they could not use because it was old or contained diseases that won't harm us. The Red saw me as undermining everything they stood for."

"I should tell Jo about this," Harry said. "This is something the HDU should definitely be aware of."

"No! No, we will deal with it. We vampires can police our own, just as I dealt with the vampire who turned you, we will deal with them. Jo Burns would want to wait for them to commit a crime. She's still a police officer at heart and wants evidence. We can act without hinderance."

"But we don't know how many of them there are, or if they've killed or will kill. Jo needs to know this before it becomes a problem."

"This is hard for you, Harry, but you must understand. You have kept your human job, but you are not human. Your loyalty must lie with your kind."

"A part of me still is human, and I signed on for my job to protect humans. I'm going to tell Jo."

Before the Countess could argue further, Harry changed into bat form and flew away, leaving his clothes to fall to the floor of the Countess' office.

Senior Agent Jo Burns woke to a scratching on her bedroom window. A bat was outside.

"Harry?" She asked, still half asleep.

The bat nodded, which was not a thing she'd ever seen a bat do before.

She opened the window, and Harry flew in.

Jo grabbed a dressing gown, and threw it on the bed, then went to the lounge room, while Harry returned to his human form.

Jo, in her pink fluffy winter pyjamas, reflected that she'd never anticipated a junior agent being in her home, wearing her cat patterned dressing gown.

Harry told her the story. Jo gave him a notebook and he drew the logo of The Red.

"Do you have clothes at the office?" Jo asked. He nodded.

Jo went back to her room and changed, and drove to the HDU office, with Harry in the passenger seat.

Jo called Agent Marissa Tyler, and Trainee Agent Kate Murdoch, and asked them to come in as well. Harry, now dressed in clothes he kept in his locker, told the story again.

"And the Countess really didn't want you to report this?" Jo clarified.

"No. It was like some kind of loyalty test. I had to keep it quiet and help her hunt them down, instead of telling you."

"Did you tell her where you saw this fang?"

"I just told her it was a club. But it was the same club where I was bitten, where she rescued me, so she will probably guess."

"Well, let's see if we can beat her to finding him." Jo said. "Because I want information. I want to know how many of them there are and just what a danger they are to the humans in this city."

They went to the club. Harry showed them where the vampire bumped into him.

Jo looked at Kate, hopefully.

"You're kidding? With this many scents?" Kate asked.

"I don't know. I don't know how the world smells to you. If you can't do it, you can't do it. We'll just spread out and look."

"Wait. I can smell two vampires. One's Harry, one went off this way." Kate led the way into the club, across the dance floor, and out another door into a back alley. She continued walking, finally stopping at a hotel. "He's gone in, and not come out."

They entered the hotel, and Kate led them to a lift.

"How do we deal with this?" Harry asked?

"We stop on every floor," Jo answered.

On the ninth floor, Kate picked up the scent again, and led them to a room.

Jo knocked.

A man answered.

"That's him," Harry said.

"You didn't need to bring all your friends," the vampire said. "But do come in, all of you."

They entered the room.

"What's your name?" Jo asked.

"Call me Alexander. And you are the head of the Human Defence Unit, Senior Agent Burns, if I'm not mistaken."

"You're well informed," Jo said.

73

"I've been following your young friend. I needed to contact you, but I thought you might react badly to a strange vampire simply approaching you."

"You thought right. I've been informed you're part of an organisation that believes vampires should be free to hunt. That makes you a threat to my city."

"Your city?" He laughed. "You've been misinformed. I am here to warn you about a vampire who is turning your citizens under your nose, as she turned me, and hundreds of others. If she is not stopped you will hardly have any humans to defend."

"Who is she?" Harry asked.

"You should know. She turned you."

"No, the fang who turned me is dead. Countess Anastasia Arafami killed her."

"You remember that, do you?"

"I don't remember it," Harry was now hesitant. "The Countess told me."

"Of course the Countess told you. She told me something similar. She told my friends similar things as well. Then we caught her in the act of turning another person we knew. We tried to kill her, but she is old and strong. Only three of us survived. We followed her around the world. We called ourselves The Red, a reminder of the blood we're forced to drink. We have always avoided human blood, feeding from livestock instead. We caught up with her in Paris five years ago, I was the only one of my group to survive."

"I know the Countess. She is the one I negotiated a deal with, that vampires in this city wouldn't feed on humans, and we would leave them alone."

"Vampires in this city. Tell me, were there vampires here before she arrived? Has the community in her house been growing?"

"Well, yes, we're getting more vampires all the time," Harry began, "but... oh..."

"Oh, indeed," Jo said. "Now we have a problem of who to believe. We need evidence. In the meantime, I think I would feel better if you were in custody."

Alexander didn't argue or fight, and was soon locked in a cell. As the agents were leaving him, he called Harry back.

"Harry," he said. "There is so much folklore about people like us. Stories such as sunlight will kill us, but I'm sure you've found out that it just causes an intense sunburn very quickly. So I wonder, what do you think of the story that if the vampire who turned you is killed, you can become human again?"

"I don't know," Harry said. "I don't think anything of it."

"Maybe you should. I think about it all the time."

At the Countess' house, they found signs she had packed and left quickly. The other resident vampires appeared to have gone with her. There was blood poured all around the house.

"What can you smell?" Jo asked Kate.

"Blood, just blood," Kate answered. "It's everywhere."

The fridge in the kitchen had been emptied and the contents of numerous blood pouches spread around the whole house.

"Sorry, I told her Kate was a wolf. I thought I could trust her," Harry said. "I guess she knew to mess up the scent."

"We will put an alert out for police to be on the look out for her, and alert Border Force as well." Jo said. "And I guess we release Alexander. There's no point in holding him."

"You trusted her, too, didn't you?" Harry asked quietly.

"I always knew she'd follow her own interests. I just made the mistake of thinking I knew what those interests were."

Human

Agent Harry Smythe was on patrol, flying high over the city.

It had initially been difficult coming to terms with becoming a vampire, but now he had learned to use his abilities to his benefit.

As a bat, his vision wasn't great, but inbuilt sonar allowed him to "see" everything below.

Brisbane had changed since Countess Anastasia Arafami and her group of vampires had left. It was much quieter. As far as Harry could tell, he was the only vampire left in Brisbane.

As he flew, he recalled what Alexander had told him: that there was a belief that if the vampire who had turned him was killed, he could become human again. He wondered if he would have killed the Countess if he had found her.

Alexander was the last of a group called The Red, vampires turned by the Countess, who had sworn to kill her. He was the last, because the Countess was strong and ancient, and her creations were no match for their creator. Alexander had offered to take Harry with him. Harry had turned the offer down, feeling he would do more good in his HDU role.

So while the Countess was still on the run with her whole household of newly-minted loyal vampires, Harry was still patrolling the skies of Brisbane, looking out for any threats to the unknowing, sleeping city.

He was over the South Bank cultural precinct when he felt the pain. He flapped wildly somersaulting in the sky as he felt an extreme stabbing pain in his chest. For a moment, he thought he was having a heart attack, but vampires were immune to such things.

The pain spread through his whole body, as he failed to keep himself in flight, and plummeted to the ground.

He curled in excruciating pain, and began vomiting blood. Involuntarily, he resumed the human form.

In human form, he lay, naked, screaming in pain, and vomiting copious amounts of blood.

That was how he was found, by group of horrified people who were walking from the theatre to the railway station.

Somewhere in the pain, Harry registered the flashing lights of the ambulance, then he knew nothing more except pain, darkness and vomiting.

Senior Agent Jo Burns was woken by a call from Agent Marissa Tyler, who was supervising the night shift.

"Harry was supposed to be back from patrol hours ago, but there's no sign of him. I don't know what he found or what trouble he's got into."

"I'm coming in," she said.

Jo decided the first course of action would be to check police activity for the night, before checking hospitals, and then walking the planned route of Harry's flight.

"What if something happened to him in bat form?" Marissa asked. "How do we find a bat lost in the city?"

"Let's hope we don't have to do that," Jo said.

They began with police reports for the night. There was nothing, but the police were not known for doing their reports in a timely manner, so even if something was amiss they might not hear about it until the next day.

Then they divided up the hospitals in the city and began phoning, posing as police officers looking for a missing person.

When Marissa called the Royal Brisbane Hospital, she was told an unknown man had been brought into the Emergency Department naked, vomiting blood and apparently in extreme pain. He'd been in no condition to talk.

"I'll go," Jo said. "You stay here, in case it's not him and he calls."

It was not long before Jo called to advise Marissa the mystery patient was Harry.

Jo presented police credentials, which were among many different forms of identity she carried, and was allowed to stay by Harry's bedside, saying he was under arrest.

"We don't know what's wrong with him," a doctor said. "His heart rate, blood pressure, temperature, everything, is all over the place."

Harry was a vampire. He shouldn't have had a heart rate, blood pressure. His temperature should have been room temperature. Now he had a raging fever.

"I need to call in a specialist," Jo said.

"Only if they've got privileges here," the doctor replied.

"In that case I'm taking him, transferring him to another facility," Jo said.

"I'm not going to authorise that," the doctor replied.

"You're not getting a choice," Jo responded.

She called Marissa and ordered her to get an ambulance and have the HDU pathologist Helen Thompson waiting. She explained Harry's situation as best she could while the doctor was listening: "He's got a raging fever, blood pressure keeps going up and down, heart rate speeds up and slows down. We're going to need Helen ready with everything possible to deal with it."

"But he doesn't have blood circulating. He's a vampire, he…"

"Exactly. Helen's our expert. Let's get him to her as fast as possible."

In less than an hour, Harry was lying in the pathology lab of the HDU. Helen briefly pointed out that she normally dealt with the dead rather than the living, before sedating Harry, placing a drip in his arm, and putting him into a MRI machine to check brain activity.

"I think your guess was right," Helen eventually told Jo. "He's turning back into a human. His whole body is changing. I don't think there's anything we can do for him but keep him comfortable. He's brought up most of the blood he's ingested in the last day or so, so now that's clear, there's nothing else to do. I'm keeping him sedated until he stabilises. The hospital probably could have done the same, but they would have wasted time trying to work out what was wrong with him."

It was two days before Harry was free of the pain, and Helen withdrew the pain control.

A day later he was starting to eat regular food, and another fortnight before Helen cleared him to work.

Despite being cleared, Harry felt strange. He'd taken ages to adapt to being a vampire, and now felt completely lost being human again.

Bloodstone

Senior Agent Jo Burns sat at the table of the coffee shop, facing the door, slowly sipping her coffee as she waited for him to arrive.

When Alexander entered, she barely recognised him. He was a grey-haired old man, when he'd appeared to be in his mid-twenties the last time she'd seen him.

"Agent Burns, thank you for meeting me," he said as he sat opposite her.

"I didn't expect to see you back in Brisbane," she answered. "But I know your quest was successful."

He gave a waitress his order. Then turned back to Jo. "How is friend Harry?"

"He's finding the transition challenging."

"I am not surprised. I see the way you look at me. Yes, this is the age I am naturally. Being human again has come with the difficulties of age. I would have come here sooner, if my health had allowed it."

"Why are you here now?"

With slightly shaking hands, he took a gold chain from his neck. Attached to it, having been tucked inside his shirt, was a pendant with what appeared to be a massive ruby.

"Do you know about bloodstones?" he asked.

"No."

"When you kill a vampire, their body ages to the point they would have naturally aged, just as returning to being a human has aged me. You have seen this, I'm sure."

Jo nodded.

He continued: "When you kill an old vampire, hundreds or more years old, they turn to dust, because that is the condition they would have been naturally."

Jo nodded again. She hadn't seen it, but she could understand the concept.

Alexander continued his story: "When you kill an ancient vampire, a thousand or more years old, among the dust will be a red stone. It is known as a bloodstone. In the right hands, or perhaps I should say the wrong hands, a bloodstone can be used to resurrect the vampire. This is the Countess' bloodstone. I had it made into a pendant so I could carry it. Among the people she turned are some who are not happy to be human again. There are also some other ancient vampires who want their Countess back. I am too old and feeble to protect this stone. That is why I am giving it to you."

He put the necklace on the table, got up and walked away.

Jo sat staring at the pendant, as the waitress came with Alexander's coffee.

Jo swept the pendant into her handbag, and asked for the bill.

Two days later the Human Defence Unit was called to a crime scene. Jo was accompanied by Trainee Agent Kate Murdoch. The HDU's police contact Inspector David Webber told Jo, "It's an old man, with no ID, looks like his throat was torn out. He had your business card in his pocket."

A quick look told Jo it was Alexander, and he had been killed by a vampire.

Kate said: "He smells like Harry, human, but with a slight hint of vampire. I smell vampires, as well, at least three of them were here."

"Who was he?" David asked.

"He was the vampire who killed the Countess, and freed Harry, as well as himself and many others."

"This old man? He doesn't look like someone who would have been a threat to vampires."

"He's only old because he's human again. As a vampire, he was young."

"So why would other vampires come after him? He wasn't dangerous to them any more."

"They were after something. They didn't get it."

"How do you know?"

"Because he gave it to me."

"So they will come after you?"

"Possibly. If they work out who he gave it to."

"Like if they found your card on him, the same as I did?"

"Like that, yes."

"What are you going to do?"

"I'm going to investigate the crime. Track down the vampires, before they track me down. I have an entire secret organisation for that purpose, after all."

"I want to help."

"It's not a police matter."

"It's a personal matter."

"We're not married any more, remember?"

"I remember. I'm still helping."

It was a simple plan, a trap. Jo was the bait.

Jo wore the pendant around her neck, in full view. She went out to dinner, accompanied by David. They ate, left the restaurant and went for a walk, choosing quiet streets, talking, acting unaware of the shadows following them.

Some of the following shadows were HDU members, all armed with mini crossbows which had wooden bolts. This had been found the most effective way of staking vampires from a distance. They also carried ultraviolet laser pointer type lights. Jo and David were similarly armed, Jo's weapons in her handbag which she kept unfastened, and David's in pockets and tucked inside his jacket.

Other following shadows, were not friendly.

Jo looked at David and raised an eyebrow. He gave a slight nod. They were both aware they were being stalked, and had a fair idea of which shadows were which.

They turned from the dimly lit road down into a less well lit alley. It looked like a casual turn. It was anything but.

As they entered the alley, two of the following shadows sped past them to the darkest part of the alley. Another behind them began to chase them, trying to force them into a trap.

Jo clicked a device in her jacket pocket. Suddenly floodlights lit up the alley.

The surrounding vampires found themselves surrounded.

"We're not taking prisoners," Jo announced.

Crossbow bolts were fired. All of the fangs had been old. They were dust in moments. Jo checked the piles of dust and found two had left bloodstones.

"What will you do with them? You can't risk them being found by someone who knows what they are," David said.

"There's nowhere safer than a place that doesn't exist," Jo replied. "They'll be fine secured in the HDU office."

Sulphur

"Well that's a new one on me," Senior Agent Jo Burns said, looking down at the vaguely human-shaped pile of yellow dust, noticing the grass around it was dead and burned.

Trainee Agent Kate Murdoch gagged. "Rotten egg. Sometimes having a super-sensitive nose isn't helpful."

"Sulphur," Jo said, "Can't see why anyone would bury someone in it. It's weird, but I'm not really sure it's a case for us. We'll check it out, probably hand it back to the police. You go back to the office if the smell's too much, and send Harry out. Send Helen and Andrew as well to pick up the body."

Kate gratefully left, while Jo searched the surrounding area, and found nothing of use, no sign of a killer, human or otherwise.

When Agent Harry Smythe arrived, with Pathologist Helen Thompson, and her assistant Andrew Harrison, Jo directed them to sift through the pile of sulphur, to gather any evidence in it.

There was nothing but the yellow powder until they dug down to the body.

In the man's pocket, they found his wallet, giving his name and address.

Jo and Harry left the pathology team to continue dealing with the scene and the body, while they went to advise the victim's wife.

Using fake police ID, they introduced themselves to the man's wife.

The first thing Jo noticed about Mary Rivers, was a huge black eye, and the plaster cast on her arm.

"I'm sorry to have to tell you this, Mrs Rivers, but your husband Bill's body has just been found."

The woman nodded and sat down. "How did he die?"

"We're still trying to work that out."

She hung her head and said, "I didn't think she would do it."

"You didn't think who would do what?"

"My son's teacher. She saw the bruises on my son, and on me. Yesterday, when I went to pick him up, she pulled me aside and asked if I wanted her to stop Bill."

"You think she killed him?"

"She said weird things then. She said there was a fee."

"A fee. You paid your son's teacher to kill your husband?"

"No. She said she was a demon, and the fee was a soul."

"You agreed to give your soul to kill your husband?"

"No. She said she'd take his soul. She said he deserved it."

"Let me get this straight, your child's teacher claimed to be a demon, and said she'd kill your husband, and take his soul in payment? That's what you're saying?"

"Yes. I didn't really believe her. Or I don't think I believed her. I mean people don't really say that type of thing do they? I didn't think she really would kill him, but he always said he'd kill me if I tried to leave, especially if I tried to take little Billy away. Will I go to jail now? What will happen to Billy?"

"Well, I'm not arresting you now. I don't know a story like that even counts as soliciting someone to commit murder. Pretty sure no jury's ever going to believe you took her seriously. I will need the teacher's name and the school, though."

At the school, they were advised Billy's teacher, Miss Pritchard, had not appeared for work that day, but the principal was happy to cooperate with the police and gave Jo the teacher's home address.

Jo sent Harry to watch the back door as she knocked on the front.

The back door flew open and a young woman almost, carrying a large backpack and another bag, ran into Harry.

"Let me go," she said, quietly. "You know you want to. He deserved it. They all deserve it. I'm saving women and children. Saving them from torture. You know what torture is, I see your soul. I know what was given to you and taken from you. Let me go, then go free yourself."

Harry nodded, and let her go. She jumped the back fence, ran off through the rear neighbour's yard and disappeared from view.

Jo knocked a couple more times. Then she walked around to the back.

"No answer," she said.

"Back door's open," he answered.

They entered the house, saw drawers and the wardrobe hanging open, signs of someone packing hastily.

"She's definitely gone," Jo said. "We can ask all the regular agencies to look out for her."

"Yeah," Harry said, "but the person she killed was a horrible person, and she was protecting a woman and a kid, so maybe…"

"Maybe we don't put a lot of effort into finding her?"

"Mmm."

"We don't really want supernatural vigilantes running around. But it's only this once that we know of."

"Yeah, it was an extreme situation."

Jo thought about her daughter Katie, who had been murdered, and how she had killed the monster which had done it. "We'll put out the request to all the regular agencies, tomorrow, maybe the next day, won't flag it as urgent."

Harry

Agent Harry Smythe had had a rough couple of months.

First he's been turned to a vampire. It was a painful and horrible process.

While he struggled to adjust to that reality, he's grown to depend on the Countess, an ancient fang who had saved him from the one who had attacked and turned him. She'd taught him how to adapt to life as a vampire in the modern world, drinking blood from the blood bank rather than hunting his own food.

Then he'd discovered the Countess herself had been the one who turned him, not only that, she'd turned many other people into vampires as well. A secret society of vampires she had created were hunting her, but only one of those survived. The Countess had fled the city to escape that one vampire.

When he was suddenly returned to his human, amid more horrible pain, he knew the Countess had been killed.

Although Senior Agent Jo Burns had offered Harry as much leave as he needed to adapt, he'd insisted he keep on working. That was how he'd come to know the Countess' bloodstone was kept locked in Jo's office. A bloodstone was left when an ancient vampire was killed and the rest of the vampire turned to dust.

Harry was working the night shift. It was quiet and he was in the office alone.

A couple of storeys below him, some of the beings who lived in at the office were asleep in the staff units. In the cells, three werewolves, including Trainee Agent Kate Murdoch were spending the night safe in the knowledge they wouldn't harm anyone this full moon.

Jo's office was electronically locked, but Harry had pocketed the Open Sesame card instead of returning it to stores after his last case. The card opened any electronic lock. It was the kind of thing that organisations that didn't actually exist kept.

He swiped the card, hearing the gentle "click" of the door unlocking.

In a nearby suburb, Jo turned over in her sleep. She was dreaming. Her daughter, in a red cape was running down the hall between the cells at the HDU. "Doggies, Mummy!" she squealed. "He's going to hurt the doggies. He's not who he was and he's going to hurt the doggies."

Jo jolted awake. Dreams about Katie usually meant something, and this one was at the HDU office. Tonight there were wolves in the cells. Could those, in a little ghost girl's mind, be doggies?

Jo rang the office, and got no answer. There'd been so little happening in the city since the Countess' departure, she'd felt comfortable leaving Harry alone on duty for the night. She tried Harry's mobile phone and still had no answer. Going to her gun safe she chose what weapon to take. Not silver bullets, these "doggies" didn't deserve to be put down, they were being responsible. She loaded the tranquilliser gun with darts. What else might be trying to hurt the wolves? She should grab everything she could. While driving into the office she called her second in command Agent Marissa Tyler.

Harry used a lock pick to force open Jo's locked file cabinet. He searched through each drawer until he found the locked metal box he was looking for. He used the lock picks again, and opened the box.

Inside were three large red jewels, like highly polished rubies. He knew which one was the Countess' bloodstone. It was set in a gold pendant on a chain.

He took that stone, laid it gently on Jo's desk. From his pocket he took a knife, cut his hand, and dripped his own blood on the stone.

"Countess, return to life," he said.

Smoke curled where the blood touched the stone. Then there was a huge flash of light, and the Countess stood in front of him. Harry opened a bag he'd brought with him, and took clothes from it to give her. She dressed quickly, then picked up the other two bloodstones and put them in her pocket.

"You want to come with me?" she asked Harry.

He nodded.

She bit his throat.

Jo pulled into the car park. She considered waiting for Marissa, but decided against it. The wolves in the cells were under her protection, and if they were in danger, or a danger to someone else, she had to act.

"Jo is a very efficient hunter of things like us. We must create a distraction to slow her down before we leave," the Countess said.

Harry told her about the wolves in the cells, and that in the quarters below them both the Yowie and Andrew Harrison were sleeping.

"They will do."

The vampires went to the cells and unlocked the doors, leaving them open. Inside the wolves were backed up against the wall, hair raised, snarling at the vampires. Even in their lupine state, the wolves knew vampires meant danger.

Harry called Andrew and said there was a problem in the cells, his strength and that of Yowie were needed to try to get things under control.

Based on Katie's warning, Jo ran straight for the cells.There she found Andrew and Yowie both physically struggling with the freed werewolves.

In three quick shots, Jo tranquilliser the wolves. She checked her non-verbal staff members for bites, and then had them help her return the sleeping wolves to the cells.

The Countess and Harry had hidden as Jo ran past. Now they ran toward the exit.

They were almost at the door as Marissa entered.

Like Jo, Marissa had come with weapons for practically anything. From one of multiple holsters, she grabbed a miniature crossbow, designed to fire wooden bolts into vampire hearts, as a means of delivering a wooden stake without getting too close. She fired at the Countess and missed, was reloading as Harry leapt at her. She managed to fire the crossbow into his heart just as his teeth tore into her throat.

The Countess fled.

Harry was dead, and Marissa barely alive when Jo, Andrew and the Yowie found her. Andrew, immediately administered first aid to Marissa, tearing a piece off his pyjama shirt to use as a bandage and applying pressure to stop the bleeding.

Marissa managed to gasp, "Countess," and then lost consciousness.

Fangs

HDU Senior Agent Jo Burns sat on a bench at South Bank and looked across the river to the city centre. All of that life, she mused, all of those people who lived oblivious to the horrors that existed in their city.

Retired Senior Agent Kurt Davison approached and sat quietly beside her.

"I went to the hospital," he said quietly. "Marissa's still unconscious."

"Massive blood loss and shock," Jo answered. "She's had ten bags of blood. They say now it's just wait and see."

"She's tough. Always was."

"Did I mess up, Kurt? Should I have seen that Harry wasn't coping?"

"How would you have seen it? Did he say anything? Do anything? Tell you he was struggling?"

"No. But still. I mean I asked if he wanted time off, and he said he was fine. Maybe we need a psychologist on staff for the extreme stuff that happens."

"A psychologist? Great idea.Where are you going to find one who doesn't have every member of the team committed just for what they do in an ordinary day?"

Jo allowed herself a slight smile. She sighed. "Now, I've got the Countess loose, probably with two other ancient fangs, and I'm down two team members. This city isn't going to know what hit it."

"Do you think the Countess will stick around? She's not already half way across the world?"

"Well, of course, I can't be sure. But I've made the mistake of thinking I knew how she would act before, and I've been wrong. I have to assume she's here, because she might be. If I'm wrong, that's great, but I can't count on it."

"That makes sense. You've underestimated her before. You're an idealist. I hear you have a wolf and a zombie on the team now, and you had the fang who turned and turned against you."

"Just continuing on your tradition. You are, after all, the one who hired a Yowie, instead of putting it down or relocating it to a less populated area."

'Oh but the Yowie's just an animal. It doesn't have the brains of things that used to be human. Those you can't trust."

Jo thought of Kate Murdoch, and Andrew Harrison, and even Harry when he'd learned to cope as a vampire and then couldn't handle the sudden change back to humanity. "No, those I have been able to trust. What I couldn't trust were outside forces, such as the Countess."

"Sometimes, I wonder if the fight was ever worth it," Kurt said quietly.

"Of course it was worth it. There's a city full of human beings who are safe, who don't even know the world we know. Surely that's worth something. Where does this come from? Regretting your choices now you've retired?"

"No, just regretting getting old. But then, that's optional isn't it? We both know creatures who we could bargain with to stop aging."

"Oh, but at what cost? What would be worth losing your humanity for?"

"No pain. No aging. No niggling annoyance from bones that broke years ago. Yeah I think so."

He was fast. He turned towards her, grabbed both her arms, and went to bite her neck.

A child's voice from nowhere yelled, "No!"

Kurt was sent flying through the air, landing impaled through the heart on a tree branch.

"Katie!" Jo called.

"More bad people. Mummy run!" Katie's voice came from the air.

Jo ran, while digging in her handbag for the miniature crossbow and wooden bolts she always carried with her now.

A group of people walking down the bougainvillea pathway turned and started to run after her. Another group of people got up from a table outside the central cafes and joined the chase.

While still running, Jo tried to count, she thought there were about eight fangs after her.

She could turn to fire, but she couldn't get off eight bolts before the fangs caught up.

Then she saw them, running towards her from the other direction; her ex-husband David Webber, Trainee Agent Kate Murdoch, Andrew Harrison and the Yowie. They were all armed with miniature crossbows. As soon as they were in range, they all began firing. Jo turned and joined them.

It was over in moments. Vampires were dead all around them.

"How did you know to come?" Jo asked.

"Katie called me. I called everyone else," David answered.

"Katie again. She saved me. Kurt Davidson was a fang. He went into it knowingly, to avoid getting old," Jo said.

She looked around at the group of people who had come to rescue her. "Thanks everyone, including you, Katie, wherever you are."

A little girl's giggle filled the air for a moment.

Jo continued: "David, if we didn't need you as our police liaison I would offer to recruit you right now. Kate, you're promoted to full agent. Andrew, if you want to come out of the pathology lab and be an agent temporarily, until the crisis is over, you're hired, you too, Yowie, if you want, although I don't know how I'll explain you on the streets."

The Yowie reached down and patted her on the head.

"Since you're normally the clean-up crew, I guess we're all helping you with this clean-up. Tomorrow, I'm going to try to get more experienced agents to transfer from other capital cities. We're at war everyone. The Countess clearly didn't leave and she's not even pretending to play by the rules this time. The city's going to be overrun with fangs."

Memories

The funerals were over. Jo had convinced both Harry's parents and Kurt's wife, of the wisdom of cremation. She'd even suggested where to scatter their ashes, scatter being the important part.

She hoped her colleagues were able to rest in peace, a thing never completely guaranteed with vampires.

Jo sat in her office remembering both Kurt and Harry, and how they had become a part of her life.

It had begun with Katie.

Jo had been a police officer. After time as a detective, she'd gone back to uniform after her maternity leave. She'd been allowed to stay on day shift if she went back to uniform, so that was the deal. That way Katie could go to Day Care and Jo could go back to work.

Having had her career on hold for a year, her husband, David, who had gone through the police academy with her had been promoted ahead of her. She tried not to be jealous. After all, Katie was worth it.

Each day, she would take Katie to day care, and go on to the Roma Street station from there to clock in for work. At the end of the day, she'd go pick Katie up, and hear all about her day, as they drove home.

On the day that changed everything, Day Care was having a costume party, and Katie was dressed as Red Riding Hood.

When Jo clocked out that day, she'd entered her code at the Day Care Centre to get in, and found the carers tied up, the children missing. She untied the centre manager, ascertained the offender had just left and which way staff watching through the large window had seen him go, with tiny children in sacks. Jo and left the manager to free her staff, and ran after the offender, while calling on her radio for back up.

She caught up, found someone in a strange hairy costume, with pointed ears and horns, hanging wiggling sacks on a tree.

She drew her service weapon and called out for the offender to freeze. The call was unheeded, so she fired, hitting the offender in the back of the head.

As other police officers arrived, the offender lay bleeding out, while Jo pulled down the sacks and released the children. Twenty toddlers were safely released from the sacks, but one, her Katie, was dead.

That day, Jo had sat, after reporting to her superiors, on a bench seat in a hallway in the station, not knowing what to do.

A man she didn't know, sat beside her.

"A Krampus," he said, quietly. "That's the word for the thing you killed this afternoon. You took it down with a single shot. That's impressive. I'm sorry for your loss, but you saved a lot of children from a monster today, and there are more monsters out there. I know you'll take time off after this, but when you're ready, I want you to consider transferring to my unit, where you can learn what's really out there."

He gave her a card which identified him as Senior Agent Kurt Davison of the Human Defence Unit.

Three months later, with her marriage failing as Jo and David's grief pulled them apart, Jo joined the unit.

Kurt made it clear he was training Jo to be his replacement, as he was approaching retirement age. The other person Jo worked most closely with was then Trainee Agent Marissa Tyler. Marissa's pet project then was a Yowie. She was teaching it to work as an office cleaner, and some nights taking it out so it could run in its native bush land.

In time, Kurt had retired, Jo had taken over as Senior Agent, Marissa had been promoted to full agent, and Jo had taken on a new trainee Harry Smythe.

Harry had been hired on the basis of potential Jo had seen, not already having particular skills. He'd been enthusiastic, and an avid learner, always amazed at the new things he learned about the world hidden from most of society.

Harry had been through hell, hexed by a witch, turned by a vampire, betrayed by a mentor, unexpectedly turned human again. He'd been unable to cope, and had resurrected the vampire who'd originally turned him, so she could turn him back into a fang.

He'd attacked Marissa, and she'd killed him in self defence, being injured so badly herself that a week later she was still in a coma.

In the aftermath, Jo had turned to Kurt to help her deal with everything. Kurt was also then a fang, and Jo was saved from his attack by Katie's ghost.

Jo went over and over it all in his mind.

She wasn't sure she'd ever got over the pain of losing Katie. Even now, she regularly dreamed of chasing Katie, always in her Red Riding Hood cloak, but never catching her. These other losses on top of that were unbearable. Like Katie, Harry and Marissa were her responsibility, and she felt she'd let them down.

The tears flowed freely, as she sat at her desk, staring at the opposite wall, remembering.

How much was too much? Would this overwhelming misery end her career, or worse? Would she end up doing something as self-destructive as Harry had done? What if Marissa died? How would she cope with that?

Her reverie was interrupted by a knock on the office door.

Trainee Agent Kate Murdoch said, "Sorry to interrupt, boss. But you're going to want the news. Helen just got a call from the hospital. Marissa's awake. They say she's going to be OK."

Jo slowly dabbed her tears and blew her nose. She took a deep breath, hoping her voice wouldn't quaver. "OK," she said. "Let's go see her."

Playing the Queen

HDU Senior Agent Jo Burns and Police Inspector David Webber were talking in the foyer of the Roma Street Police Station.

Jo was there waiting to meet two new transfers from the New South Wales HDU.

A woman Jo recognised as journalist Kerry Perry walked in the front door, saw Jo and approached her.

"Hi Sergeant Burns," she said.

Kerry had done the police rounds for a small local paper for years. Most local police knew her. Jo didn't dislike her, but was very wary about what she could say to any journalist.

"Hi, Kerry. It's not Sergeant any more. I quit the force after my daughter was murdered. I'm just a civilian now. I work down in the basement, in payroll." Apart from the bit about being "just a civilian," and "working in payroll,"it was true. The best lies were hidden behind a wall of truth.

"That's weird, because I had a call about you the other day."

"About me?"

"Yes, this woman was accusing you of police harassment. I thought that was weird, because, I haven't seen you for a long time, but you always had a reputation as a straight shooter. But this woman, Anastasia Arafami, told this story about how you had ordered police to search for her because of a personal grudge, when she hadn't been charged with any crime."

"The Countess contacted you?" Jo was mystified.

"Countess?"

Of course actually acknowledging she knew the woman was a mistake. How would she cover for that? "Most cops know the Countess. Sometimes she's European aristocrat. Sometimes she's a thousand year old vampire. She's only dangerous when she's off her meds. If she is off her meds, stay away from her. Can I suggest you not publish anything about her? You wouldn't want it to look like your paper was exploiting a psych patient."

David decided to throw a rescue line. He said, "Actually, we are looking for the Countess at the moment. She was in a secure psych ward and escaped. Her psychiatrist says she really should be back in for her own safety. If you know where she's hiding, you'd actually be helping her if you told me."

"Yeah, telling police how to find someone who claims they're being unfairly targeted by police doesn't seem a great idea, protecting sources and all that. Thanks for that though, Inspector. Sergeant, or I guess it's Ms Burns now, I really thought if any woman was going to break the glass ceiling here, it would be you. I never expected to see you just give it up, but that whole thing with your daughter was just messed up, and you saved all those other kids. It wasn't fair."

"No. It was far from fair."

"I had trouble writing that. I don't know how you managed to live through it. That man was a monster. Sorry. I know you knew that."

A monster? Yes the killer had been a monster; the first actual monster Jo had ever seen.

"Anyway," the reporter continued, "I hope they're treating you well in payroll, and I'm sorry that happened to you."

She left them. Once she was out of earshot, Jo said to David, "What the hell was that about? Why would the Countess risk revealing herself by talking to the media?"

David was thoughtful a moment. "I think it's like chess."

"You know I don't like chess."

"Still, go with the metaphor here. The queen's the most powerful piece. She's their queen, and you're ours. She wants to get the opposite queen off the board. Trying to get at your reputation, have you exposed in the media as crooked. But she found a journo who actually knows your story, and apparently respects you. If she tries another one, the lid could be blown off everything. Everyone would know about monsters, and how the small group of people is that's protecting the world from them."

"Doesn't the queen protect the king? Who's the king in your analogy?"

"On our side? The city. The state. Humanity. Everything you've fought to protect since Katie died. On her side? The vampire community she wants to build. The one she was building before she was taken out before."

"Well, if it's chess we're playing, with Kurt and Harry dead, and Marissa still on sick leave, I think we've lost enough pieces. Let's find a way to win this game."

Later that day, while Jo was showing her new members of staff around the HDU offices, David received a call from Kerry Perry.

Anastasia Arafami had called her again. This time she had said both that she was a countess, and that she was a vampire, and would kill Kerry if the story about Jo did not run. Kerry didn't know where the Countess was, but she had a phone number, which she passed on to David.

David called Jo. He couldn't trace a mobile phone without a warrant, but Jo could.

Jo called a meeting, with David, Agent Kate Murdoch, recently inducted Temporary Agent Andrew Harrison, the Yowie, and the two transferees, Agents Scott Cooper, and Elizabeth Jones.

Jo caught everyone up to date.

"From what happened with Harry, we know that killing the Countess will mean everyone she's turned will become human again, but we also know she had the bloodstones of two other ancient vampires. If she's brought them back, they could also have turned people. We don't know how big a group of fangs we might walk into, but the first order is to take out the Countess, then go for anyone else who looks old, and anyone who we can't avoid killing."

The new agents were a bit wary of the Yowie, and of Andrew, who while no longer a slave still had his zombie strength. Andrew went with David, the Yowie with Jo, while the two new agents were with Kate. The plan was to approach from different directions, to try box in the Countess along with whatever vampires were with her.

Everyone carried intense UV laser pointers, and mini crossbows that shot wooden stakes.

As they drove, the flashing dot on the gps which indicated where the Countess' phone was, moved. All three cars adapted their journey. The Countess was going somewhere.

It was a nondescript house. Jo and Yowie took the front door, David and Andrew took the back, the others entering through a large sliding door at the side.

They moved stealthily through the house. A couple of vampires apparently on guard duty were silently despatched with hand-held stakes.

In a back room, they found the Countess, surrounded by other fangs, with Kerry Perry tied to a chair.

"Once you are a vampire, you will do as I have instructed. You will help take down Jo Burns and her team of vampire hunters. This city will belong to us."

Jo fired the crossbow. The Countess went down and turned to dust. Vampires around her began vomiting blood, and collapsing on the floor.

"They're turning back," Jo said to her team, who were all in the room now. "It looks like there aren't any other older vampires here, so we just need medical help for these. Call Helen. She's the closest thing to an expert we've got. Someone untie Kerry."

Jo dug through the dust to find a red stone. She was not going to keep the bloodstone and risk the Countess coming back this time. She pulled out her service weapon and shot the sparkling red stone, shattering it. "I want that spread over as great an area as possible," she said.

"I knew you couldn't just be down in the basement doing payroll," Kerry said.

"Sorry I lied," Jo said. "Monsters are real, and my team stops them taking over. I'm going to ask you not to write the story."

"Because everyone would freak out and there'd be mass panic?" Kerry said.

"Yes, because of that," Jo answered.

"How do I help?" Kerry asked.

Something New

"So is that a vampire or just a bat?" Kerry Perry asked as she pointed to an animal flying across the full moon.

"Bat. Probably," Senior Agent Jo Burns replied. They were sitting side by side on a bench seat at Southbank Parklands

Jo recalled that it was this same seat she'd been on when her former boss, Kurt Davison had attacked her. Now she was here, talking with a journalist. The world really had changed.

"Probably?"

"Probably. There's a lot of flying foxes or fruit bats or whatever you call them around. Even if it's a vampire, it's not a problem unless they attack someone. Lots of monsters find ways to live without harming humans."

"Good to know. Some of those people who came with you to rescue me from the Countess didn't seem quite... Was one of them some kind of ape?"

"Yowie."

"They're real?"

"That one is. The Bundamba Yowie. When his home was getting built in too much, he did a fair amount of property damage. My predecessor had the choice of relocating him to pristine bush somewhere, or bringing him in. He's normally our office cleaner, but lately he's come out when we've needed extra muscle. The guy who couldn't speak was a zombie, the spell making him a zombie was broken. He's still extra-strong, can't speak and chose to live-in at my unit rather than going home and traumatising the family who had already buried him. One of the agents with me that night was a werewolf. She's locked up in the cells tonight, voluntarily, along with a couple of other wolves. Everyone else on the team's human. Katie's not really on the team."

"Your little girl, Katie?"

"Ghost. She's saved my life a couple of times."

"Wow."

"You said you wanted to help."

"Yes."

"I've been talking to my colleagues in other states. We have a job for you if you want it. Officially, you'd be part of Police Media. That's where you tell family and friends you're working. Whenever information about one of our cases leaks into the public domain, you help us control the narrative. If the whole thing is exposed, you're our front line in reassuring people, and giving them information on how to stay safe. No HDU branch in the country ever thought this position would ever be necessary, but then the Countess approached you, and we discovered how easy it would be to expose everything."

"Public relations for a secret organisation was never a goal for me, but I see how it could be important. The Countess was scary and she was determined to make me publicise the existence of vampires."

"It's a completely new position. You would be based in our office, but might have to be sent interstate at any time if a crisis became public knowledge. If this experiment leads to media people being appointed in other states, you would be the person to teach them how to do the job. Effectively, you'd be our national head of media."

"National head of something sounds less impressive when you're the only one doing it."

"Are you in?"

"When do I start?"

Jo handed her a newspaper. "Now. You're not the only journo the Countess contacted, just the only one who refused to run her story."

105

Kerry began reading the story, "Oh no, I know this guy. He's a major…"

"Vampire."

"What?"

"Read on. He says he was turned. It wasn't the Countess, because she was dead before he claims it, but there were two other ancient vampires in town."

"So what are you going to do?"

"He's exposed vampires, and the HDU, if you read all the way through it. Tonight, we're taking him in. He's going to a secure unit, officially a mental health facility. We've got a couple of special cases there. That's if he doesn't force us to kill him instead of taking him in. If we get him without a fight, your story is that this poor deluded man is now in a secure facility for his own safety. Otherwise, it's about his disappearance, and police are looking for him, and concerned for his safety. The important thing is that people think this story is the ranting of someone who is extremely unwell. If you want the job, I can set you up with your office now, before I go to bring this guy in."

Kerry read through the whole article. "This is all really real, isn't it? I mean, we're on the brink of mass panic if we're not on top of it?"

Jo nodded.

"OK. I'm supposed to serve notice if I quit my job."

"I can pull strings to get you out of that."

"Then I guess, you can show me my office."

Jo wasn't entirely sure that bringing in a journalist was the best idea. She hadn't thought of any better way to deal with vampires outing themselves, and the HDU, in the media. Hunting down monsters in the shadows, was something she was used to. Moving the fight into the public spotlight was something entirely new.

The Countess had made the move. At least one of the two other ancient vampires out there had continued it.

Now, it was up to Jo to find a way to counter it.

Trap

It was a larger than average house. Apart from that, there was nothing to distinguish it from any of the other acreage properties in the outer suburbs.

Senior Agent Jo led half the team through the front door, the other half came in through the back.

It should have gone smoothly. The previous similar operation had been easy.

They walked quietly through darkened halls and rooms, searching for the occupant, and any other vampires he might be working with.

Both halves of the team met in the middle. Jo redirected them, Andrew, Scott and Elizabeth to search upstairs, while she, David and the Yowie, searched downstairs.

Jo was opening the pantry door when she felt a something like a insect bite on the back of her neck. Then she felt weak for a moment and everything went black.

She woke in what seemed to be a store room. All of her team were there, all unconscious. Another man was there as well, and he seemed to be just coming to. "Restrain me," he said, sounding as if his voice was coming from a great distance.

"What?" Jo's voice also sounded like it was coming from a long way away.

"Full moon. Restrain me," he said.

Something clicked. Jo reached for her handcuffs, but they were gone. She frantically started searching the room. Throwing things off shelves, in the half light.

Andrew seemed to come around next, sitting up and looking around.

"He's a wolf!" Jo said to Andrew. "Help me find something to restrain him."

Andrew got to his feet, swaying, and did something Jo could not have anticipated. His normal shambling gait exacerbated by the drugs, he lurched toward the wolf. He pushed the werewolf down and laid across his body, pinning him to the floor.

How long could a zombie hold a werewolf pinned down? Jo kept looking for something to use as a restraint. The shelves held all kinds of household odds and ends, unopened boxes of washing powder and packs of toilet paper, bulk bottles of cleaning products to be dispensed into smaller bottles for use.

David woke up, and did the sensible thing Jo hadn't thought to do. He turned on the light. That allowed them to see that the werewolf's body was already changing, flailing legs becoming hairier and changing shape.

Jo found a shelf of linen. She grabbed a sheet, twisted it, then tied it around the wolf's legs. David took another sheet, and tied the wolf's arms over his head. Andrew continued to pin the upper body, so the wolf could not get up.

The others were waking up now.

"What's happening?" Elizabeth asked.

"It was a trap," Jo said. "The fang we came for knew that we would come after he published that story. He'd already trapped a werewolf here, sedated. The wolf was able to give me a warning before it turned. Apparently they don't turn while drugged."

"So the wolf's not in on it?"

"No, just a victim. One we need to get out of here safely when we get ourselves out."

David had been examining the lock on the room. "It's electronic," he said. "No chance you've got your Open Sesame key with you?"

"The fang, or I would guess, fangs, took everything."

The Yowie looked at the lock, then put its hands over its ears. Since no-one seemed to understand, it held David's hands and put them over his hears. Then went to Jo, took her hands and put them over her ears.

"You want us to cover our ears? I guess we can do that. Everyone cover your ears."

Everyone did as instructed. On the floor, Andrew kept his body pressing down on the struggling werewolf, while covering his ears.

The Yowie went to the electronic lock and began a high pitched screech, the pitch getting higher and higher. The wolf on the floor howled and thrashed in response to the sound. Then the door swung open.

The Yowie stopped its screech.

"Do you shatter wine glasses as well?" Jo asked. The Yowie patted her on the head.

"No point in stealth. That noise will have woken everyone within a kilometre of here," David said. He found a toolbox, and looked for something useful in it. Hammers and screwdrivers might have worked against humans, but not vampires.

"Tomato stakes. I've got gardening supplies over here, including tomato stakes right at the back. They must have forgotten they were here," Scott said.

Everyone, with the exception of Andrew who was still on wolf duty, armed themselves with a stake. Jo told the Yowie to stay with Andrew, in case he needed someone to protect him. The rest of the group stayed together as they made their way out of the room.

They did not have to go far to find a group of half a dozen fangs, all curled up on the floor in pain, blood flowing from their ears.

"Looks like Yowie screeches do more than open doors," Jo said. "Stake them all, let's get this over with."

She found the fang they'd actually come for and, "Where's the one who turned you?"

"Not here. Cassius learned from the Countess' mistake. You won't find him or Marcus, just an endless number of vampires they've created. You can't win. You can't keep us secret. Kill me now, and Cassius will bring me back to life by morning."

"You think I'm leaving your body for him to revive? No I'm cremating you tonight. Long before your leader finds out you've failed, you'll already be cremated, and poured into the river, where he can't resurrect you."

She forced the stake through his heart.

"OK everyone, clean up. Someone find our gear and sedate that poor wolf. He can sleep it off in our cells. Let's get these fangs burned and scattered before they come back to bite us."

The next day's news would feature a release from the Police Media unit, that the journalist who recently claimed in a news story that he was a vampire was now missing. Police were concerned for his safety, but advised anyone who saw him not to approach.

Neighbourhood Watch

Senior Agent Jo Burns opened the cell door. The werewolf was back in human form.

"Are you OK?" she asked. "We weren't really able to check if you were injured last night. I'm sorry we were a bit rough restraining you. We were short on options. Thank you for giving me that warning."

The man answered, "You're Jo Burns aren't you? They wanted me to kill you. I told them I wouldn't. Everyone knows about you."

"What does everyone know about me?"

"That you're tough, but you're fair. You won't bother us if we don't harm humans. That you even help some of us. But if we hurt humans, you'll make sure we disappear. They wanted me to kill you. They were going to go public and say it was werewolves, not vampires that killed you. They wanted the whole world to know we exist, but to make out that they are harmless, and you were persecuting them. Everyone knows it's a lie."

"And everyone is?"

"All the werewolves I know. The vampires have been trying to recruit lots of us to join in their fight against you, because you killed someone who was important to them. None of us will join, because they're scary, but you're even more scary. But…"

"But?"

"Some of the werewolves I know have disappeared. I know they locked themselves up on the full moon, the same as I do. So it wasn't you who took them."

"So the vampires aren't just at war with the HDU. They're killing werewolves as well, and they seem to be turning lots of humans."

"It's getting scary out there. We're trying to watch out for each other, but we're just ordinary people. Well, we're ordinary people for most of the month. We don't know what we're doing."

"What if I could get an agent to work with you, like a Neighbourhood Watch set up? We help you to look out for yourselves. Help you plan a system where you all check in with each other, make sure you have contact details to call the HDU if you're in trouble."

"You can do that? I mean, your job is to defend humans, not us."

"Like you said, you're ordinary humans for most of the month."

Jo took the wolf, named Eric up to the office floor. Agent Kate Murdoch was in her office, having just showered and changed after spending the full moon in a cell.

Jo introduced them, explaining to Eric that Kate had a particular understanding of the needs of werewolves. She instructed Kate to help Eric to form a werewolf neighbourhood watch.

Then she went to Kerry's office to warn her the vampires might be stepping up their campaign to expose the whole shadow world.

Jo found Kerry fielding a call from a journalist, saying: "The guy wrote a news story saying he was a vampire, and now he's missing. Police are concerned for his safety. I only just started at Police Media, I wouldn't risk my job by speculating he was having a mental breakdown. You might be able to find a psychiatrist willing to back that theory, but I'm not saying it. The only information I have is that he is missing, and that anyone who sees him should not approach, but call police. ...

No. There's been no new information since the release. ... Yes, I know Jo Burns. She used to be a cop. She retired a few years ago. ... Super-secret spy agency? Where are you getting this? ... Well, hey, if you trust your source and can back that up... You want me to go to my superiors and say, 'You know that cop who quit after her kid was killed, is she running some kind of anti-vampire spy agency?' I only started here yesterday. That would be the shortest time in a job ever. ... If there's any follow-up on our missing journalist, I'll put out a new media release. Bye."

"The fangs are backgrounding more journalists?"

"That's the third this morning."

"It's only going to get worse. They're trying to force wolves to join them, and are apparently killing them if they don't."

"Do we have to go public?"

"Not yet. If we can get those two ancient fangs, we can turn back everyone they've turned, but we have to find them fast."

"And how do we do that?"

"I have a vague plan forming."

A Plan Comes Together

"We don't want you in any danger. You set up the meeting, but you don't go to it we do," Senior Agent Jo Burns said.

Eric, the werewolf nodded. "If this is going to keep werewolves safe, I'm in."

"As long as everything goes according to plan it will. You need to make it clear, both Cassius and Marcus have to be at the meeting, or otherwise you're walking away. You represent the werewolves, and negotiating with you is the only way they're getting wolves to join them against the HDU and me."

Eric made the call, and set up the meeting for that night.

Jo went back to her office, and briefed her team on the plan. Then, since none of them had slept the previous night, she ordered them all to get some rest.

Like most of the others, she found a bunk in the unit's rest area.

She dreamed she was running through a treed area. Ahead of her ran a little girl in a Red Riding Hood costume. "Hurry Mummy," Katie's voice called back to her. "We have to help the doggy."

Jo jolted awake.

She had a missed call from Eric on her phone. He'd left a message. The vampires had moved the meeting forward, and changed the place. It was immediately, and in a park. Since she hadn't answered his call, he would go and try to delay them until she and the team could get there.

Of course, Jo realised, ancient vampires had a tolerance for daylight.

She woke every team member who was in the HDU, and had them call the others as they drove to the meeting site.

115

"This way," Jo heard Katies voice say. She had a glimpse of red disappearing through the trees.

"This way," Jo whispered to the team.

With their mini-crossbows armed with stakes, they followed as she led the way through the trees.

They found one vampire holding Eric, the other was about to stab him with what appeared to be an ivory-handled silver sword.

For a moment, Jo hesitated, afraid of harming Eric, then she realised a wooden stake was far less harmful to him than silver was.

The next things happened in seconds, but seemed to take much more time.

Jo fired, hitting the fang with the sword. The stake hit his heart and he fell to dust.

Beside her, Kate Murdoch did the same. Kate's stake hit Eric, who collapsed. Scott Cooper fired, staking the second fang, which also turned to dust.

Jo ran over and pulled the stake from Eric's shoulder. As she watched, the wound healed. She'd known it would happen, but was still amazed watching the process.

Once she was sure Eric was fine, she scrambled amidst the dust of the ancient vampires to find two red stones. She shot both of them with her service weapon and shattered them.

"Someone pick up the shards of those bloodstones and make sure they're scattered over the widest possible area," Jo ordered. Then she turned her attention to Eric, "That was wildly courageous, and also the stupidest thing I've ever seen. What did you think would happen if I hadn't got the message?"

Eric pulled a home-made explosive device from his pocket. "I'd have used this, and taken them out with me," he said.

"Did I tell you how I became a werewolf? I was a soldier. An IED like this one injured me, and I was captured. One of the enemy was a werewolf. When I tried to escape he bit me. Did me a favour. As you've just seen, werewolves heal really well. We heal even better than this in wolf form. After the first full moon, I was strong enough to escape. After being blown up and captured, I applied for, and was granted, a discharge. A full moon would have made military life complicated."

"Do you want a job?" Jo asked.

"Thanks, but no thanks. The werewolf Neighbourhood Watch is going to keep me busy enough. We've realised that looking out for each other is going to take more than watching out for people attacking us. We need to look at how we support each other in other ways. Someone just got fired for refusing to work on night of the full moon. We need to help her get another job. Things like that are important."

"Fair enough," Jo said. "If you ever change your mind, or you need us, you know how to find us."

Bunny

Kerry Perry knocked on Senior Agent Jo Burns' office door.

"Got something weird, Jo," she said. Kerry reflected that "weird" was a relative term, especially since she was now doing public relations for an organisation the public didn't know existed.

Jo indicated the seat on the opposite side of the desk. Kerry sat.

"What is it?" Jo asked.

"A giant pink rabbit seen in the northern suburbs."

"I don't suppose we could hope it was someone celebrating Easter at the wrong time of year?"

"People who saw it close up said it had antennae, like an insect's."

Kerry handed Jo a number of news stories she'd printed off the internet.

Jo skimmed them. She noted the creature had been seen in The Gap, always near the shopping centre. No-one had claimed to have been harmed by it, only that it had walked out in front of traffic. It had been seen three nights in a row.

Jo called Marissa Tyler, who was recently back from medical leave, and Kate Murdoch, and told them they were having a night out.

Since there had been no sign the giant rabbit creature was dangerous, it would be a low-key operation. It was so low-key, in fact, that Jo had allowed Kerry Perry to tag along. The four women sat outside a restaurant in the shopping centre, watching the street. They arrived well before the time of the prior sightings, and insisted on paying when they ordered their food, not knowing if they were going to run off.

They'd just finished dessert, as a human-sized pink rabbit with antennae walked past.

"We're on," Jo said. They got up and followed the rabbit.

"This is like Alice in Wonderland," Kerry whispered, as the rabbit crossed Waterworks Road, walking in front of traffic. It was walking slowly, so the women were able to wait at the pedestrian crossing and cross with the lights, trying not to attract more attention than the rabbit was already doing.

"Definitely not human. A creature I haven't smelled before," Kate whispered.

They caught up to the creature as it was opening a gate and walking up a garden path. It didn't seem to notice them as they followed it right up to the open door.

The door opened suddenly and a woman came out, grabbed the creature by the arm and tried to hurry it into the house.

"Same smell, just human form," Kate whispered.

The woman sniffed. "Werewolf!" she screamed.

"It's OK," Jo said quietly. "We're not here to hurt you. It's just that your friend has been noticed several nights in a row. It's causing interest in the media. I guess you don't want that. We're here to help you work out what to do about it."

A tear ran down the woman's face. "My father," she said. "He had a fall, and hit his head, a week ago. He got better, but now at night time, he seems to forget himself and goes back into bunny form. I try to keep him inside, but he sneaks out while I'm getting my children ready for bed. He doesn't do any harm, I promise."

"We've been watching him. We can see he's not doing any harm, but we can also see he's behaving in a way that's likely to get him hurt, and he's drawing the kind of attention you probably don't want. I would like to suggest we get a doctor to see him."

"Doctors only deal with human physiology. They can't help us."

"Our doctor's a bit different. She's learned to treat a lot of not-quite-human patients."

Jo gave a brief explanation of the Human Defence Unit, and explained that part of defending humans was helping to keep the secret of non-human beings, so as to avoid mass panic. She told the woman about the HDU's pathologist Helen Thompson who had learned on the job to deal with multiple species' medical issues. Jo gave the woman her card, and said to call in the morning to make an appointment.

"In the meantime, first thing tomorrow, my associate here is going to release a press release that says police investigated the giant rabbit sitings, and found it to be a practical joke."

"Thank you," the woman said.

"If you need help to work on security to make sure you can keep your father inside while he's in bunny form, I can look at that for you tomorrow," Kate offered. "You've already worked out I'm a wolf. I need to be locked up on the full moon. I use the cells at work for convenience, but I've also done some modifications to my home to make sure I can be locked in if I can't get to work. Jo knows if I don't make it to the cells on the full moon, to come and let me out of the secure room at my place the next day. I can lock myself in and leave the key out of the room. So what I'm saying is, we'll help you out, whatever you need."

The woman thanked them, again, and they left.

"So did we just meet the Easter Bunny? Are Easter Bunnies real?" Kerry asked.

"I don't see why not, most things are," Marissa said.

Kerry processed the information in silence for a moment, then asked: "Is Santa Claus real?"

Marissa looked Jo's back as she walked along ahead of them. "I'll tell you about it another time," she said.

Little Birdie

A grandmother and her little grandchild were in the park. The child stopped playing in the sandpit and came to sit beside her grandmother.

"Grandma, the other kids have their mummies or daddies, not grandmas here. Why isn't my mummy here?"

"Oh, Little Birdie, your mother was very young when she hatched you. She struggled, so she flew the nest because she didn't know how to look after you. She'll come home when she's sorted herself out. For now, you're my Little Birdie, and I'm very glad to have you."

"Grandma, why can't I sing around other people. You told the kindy teacher I have a problem with my throat and can't sing, but I can. I sing with you and our friends, but you won't let me sing around other people."

"I'm sorry little bird, but we're not like other people. Bad things happen when we sing in front of other people. Our ancestors, our grandmas' grandmas' grandmas used to make ships crash by singing. Now, we live with humans, and we try not to hurt them."

"We can't really hurt people by singing, can we?"

"Oh yes, Little Birdie, we absolutely can, and you mustn't ever, ever, try it. We only sing when we're alone or just with other sirens."

The little one thought a minute, and went back to the sand pit.

A child on the swings started singing.

Before the grandmother could react, Little Birdie started singing along.

People from all over the park, as if transfixed, started to walk towards the little child.

"What a beautiful song," a woman said. "I will give you anything, anything at all if you just sing again."

The grandmother searched through her handbag for her phone and a business card with a number she'd hoped she'd never have to use.

Another woman said, "Would you like anything? Would you like an ice cream? I'm going to go and get you an ice cream."

As the grandmother dialled the number, the woman who had offered the ice cream, still in a daze, walked out to the road, aiming to cross to the shop on the other side.

The grandmother said, "Agent Burns, it's Koula Mykonos. It's happened. Little Birdie sang in public. I wasn't fast enough to stop her. Please help."

The woman on the ice cream run was hit by a car.

Koula Mykonos gave their location.

Another woman said, "Oh, she can't get your ice cream, I'll go get it for you." She began to cross the road, as traffic swerved past the accident.

While people continued to crowd around the now-frightened Little Birdie, Koula began to push her way through the crowd to get to her granddaughter.

"Get back, leave her alone. Give her space," the grandmother shouted, pushing past people. She picked up her Little Birdie. The little girl threw her arms and legs around her grandmother, and clung on, as the grandmother picked her up, and tried to push her way out of the crowd.

People pressed closer and closer, and Koula was afraid they, or others, might be crushed by the crowd.

There was a sudden screeching noise, followed by a loud static sound. People seemed to come out of their daze. In the shop, a woman who had just bought ice-cream remembered she'd left her own children unsupervised. On the road, a badly injured woman remembered her child was in the park, unsupervised.

The confused crowd dissipated, parents looking for their children, children crying for parents they couldn't see in the crowd.

Human Defence Unit Senior Agent Jo Burns pushed through the crowd that was starting to break up.

"Koula," she said. "It's going to be OK. Thanks for calling before it got too bad. Let's get you and your Little Birdie home. Some of my team are going to help sort out the crowd here."

"Are you going to kill us?" The grandmother asked quietly. "That's what you do, isn't it, when there's a threat to humans?"

"Not for accidents," Jo said, gently. "And you're not going to sing around humans again, are you, Little Birdie?"

The small girl shook her head, and hung on to her grandmother more tightly.

Jo said, "I'm really impressed with how you hold the human form, even in a crisis."

"We've had a lot of practice," Koula answered. "Everyone in our community knows the danger. We stay among the local Greek community, and try to act like other migrants, not stand out at all. This really was an accident. Little Birdie really didn't understand."

"I know. I had a little girl, too. Sometimes they learn things by making mistakes."

Jo drove the two sirens home.

On the front verandah of the house, was a young woman. She was standing beside two suitcases.

"Tina, you're home?" Koula asked.

"There were other sirens in the park. I had calls. I realised I left too much on you. I'm home to be a proper mother, and a proper daughter, if you'll both have me," Tina said.

"Of course, we'll have you. Our Little Birdie never stops asking about you."

Koula thanked Jo for her help, and took her family inside.

Phoenix

Human Defence Unit Senior Agent Jo Burns received a phone call from her police contact Inspector David Webber.

"I've got a strange one for you," he said.

"Aren't they all strange?"

"I guess they are. So, you know the communications towers on Mount Coot-tha? There's ones for all the tv stations, and for mobile phones and stuff."

"Yes."

"There's a pile of burning sticks on top of one."

"Isn't that a problem for whoever owns the tower?"

"I haven't finished yet. When their technicians went out to remove it, they were attacked by a large bird, that also appeared to be on fire."

"So, you're saying there's a phoenix nesting on a communications tower on Mount Coot-tha?"

"Yes, that's what I'm saying. I told you it was strange. I don't know how you arrest a flaming bird."

"I think with wildlife, the idea is to relocate it, but I'm not sure how to do that."

Jo called her team together to form a plan. They needed asbestos gloves, a ute, and a large asbestos mat. The Yowie would be key to the plan working.

They went as the sun was going down, planning to travel at night when there would be less traffic. They lined the tray of the ute with the asbestos mat. Then the Yowie put on his gloves.

"You're sure you're OK with this?" Jo asked. "I don't know what the bird's going to do when you're up there. If you don't want to do it, we can find another way."

The Yowie patted her on the head, and began to climb the tower.

As he neared the top, a large bird with wings that seemed to be made out of flames, dived at him. The Yowie just casually waved it away with one large hand.

"A large ape, climbing a tower, being harassed from the air. Where have I seen that before?" Jo said.

Agent Marissa Tyler laughed. "It really does look like a strange version of King Kong, doesn't it?"

The Yowie picked up the bundle of burning sticks, and carried it down the tower. The phoenix, like a magpie in September, kept swooping. The Yowie was quite comfortable, holding the tower with his feet, the nest with one hand and waving the bird away with the other hand.

"I wonder how that nest stays alight without burning up," Jo said.

"Maybe the sticks aren't burning. Maybe the phoenix is able to put some chemical on them," Marissa answered.

The Yowie brought the nest down and gently laid it on the asbestos mat in the tray of the ute. Marissa and Jo donned their asbestos gloves and helped position the nest. There was a glowing red egg in it.

"Mother bird's not going to be happy about this," Jo said.

Jo and Marissa climbed into the cab of the ute. The Yowie stayed in the tray to help keep the nest secure.

With the flaming bird following and circling, they drove an hour north toward the Glasshouse Mountains.

Not long after they reached the Bruce Highway, a police car came up behind them, lights flashing.

Jo pulled over. The car pulled in front, and a young constable got out. He looked to Jo to be about twelve, and she hadn't seen him before. He must have been in the latest batch of new recruits.

"Is something wrong, Constable?" Jo asked.

"You can't have someone in the tray of a ute," the cop said. "I'm going to have to give you a fine, and your friend's got to have another way home."

Jo pulled her police ID, one of many official IDs, from her pocket, and showed it to him. She asked, "Does that really look human to you?"

The constable looked in the tray of the ute. The Yowie froze in place. He was good at it. There was no sign even that he was breathing.

"What is that, Sergeant?" the confused constable asked Jo.

"That is evidence, we're transporting for a court case in Nambour in the morning, and since we're on overtime, we're going to have to explain this delay. You're going to be in as much hot water as we are."

The kid said, "Sorry, Sergeant." He was about to return his own car when the phoenix swooped again, screeching. The Yowie had to move to wave the bird away.

Jo said, "Get back in your car. Report to Inspector David Webber at Roma Street in the morning. He'll tell you what's going on."

As the phoenix screeched and swooped again, the Yowie once more waved the bird off. The terrified young cop ran back to his own car. Jo put the ute into gear, and pulled back out on to the highway.

They made it to their destination without further incident.

"Right," Jo said. "We need a nice bald piece of mountain top, so this can't cause a forest fire. Preferably on the side away from the local road, and where the glow isn't going to be too obvious from the highway."

128

Jo and Marissa each took a corner of the asbestos mat, The Yowie took the other two corners. They carefully carried the nest up the bushwalking path up Mount Tibrogargan. Near the top they left the path, looking for a treeless spot, with visibility obscured from the road or the path.

Eventually, they found a suitable spot, and carefully put the mat down on the ground.

The circling bird landed on the nest, settling itself on top of the egg.

"Sorry we had to disturb you, mother bird, and sorry we made you fly all that way," Jo said.

The bird screeched.

"I don't think she forgives us," Marissa said.

"I don't think I would if I were in her place either," Jo said. "We did just kidnap her baby. That's not something you just forgive." Her voice sounded harder than Marissa had ever heard it.

The Yowie pulled Jo into a bear hug.

Jo gasped for breath. "I'm fine," she said. "Let me go."

Jo walked ahead of them back to the ute.

"Yeah, she's fine," Marissa whispered to the Yowie. He patted her on the head.

Lazarus

Senior Agent Jo Burns arrived in the office of Inspector David Webber, the police liaison with the Human Defence Unit.

"Come on in, Jo. I'd like you to meet Miss Carla Johanson, who has a story I would like you to hear. Miss Johanson, Jo Burns is the police force's expert on these things."

Jo took a chair. "Hi Carla, you can call me Jo. What is it that's brought you here today?"

The young woman, looked anxious, sweaty and pale. "I'm a waitress at the Gourmet Palace, that new restaurant, in the city. My mother says I shouldn't work there, and the city is dangerous at night, but I'm in uni, and I need the money. I've never actually been scared, except when I'm actually at work. There's a man who comes in each night and just watches the patrons. He doesn't eat or drink anything, and the other staff tell me to just let him sit there. He reserves the same table in the corner every night, and never orders anything. He's pale, like milky skin, with really red lips. I dropped something near his seat the other night, and he picked it up and handed it to me. When our hands touched, his felt ice cold, like…" She paused, took a deep breath, and continued, "…like he was dead. Like there was no blood flowing."

Jo nodded slowly, and said, "So you think this man is…"

"A vampire, yes. I know it sounds silly, but that's what I think he is. I told some of the other waitresses, and they just laugh. They say he's just some crazy guy who knows the manager."

"And have you seen anything to indicate that this man has harmed anyone?"

"He's a vampire. They kill people. That's what vampires do."

"Sometimes."

"What do you mean?"

"Everyone has choices. Even if they don't have a choice in what they are, they still have a choice in what they do. Don't worry. My team and I will look into it. You just go about your normal life. If we do have to take any action against him, we won't involve you in any way."

Jo returned to the HDU offices, and asked for volunteers to go to a fancy restaurant for dinner.

That night, as Jo entered the restaurant, she saw Agents Scott Cooper and Marissa Tyler already at one table. Agents Kate Murdoch and Elizabeth Jones were at another.

"Table for one," Jo said to Carla, who happened to be the waitress who greeted her in the doorway. "Just act normally," she whispered to the nervous young woman.

As she followed Carla, she passed a table where a well-dressed, very pale man with black hair, and black eyes sat. The man stood up. "Please join me, Agent Burns," he said, very formally, with a slight trace of an accent Jo couldn't identify.

Carla looked panicked. Jo smiled at her, then said to the man, "Of course."

She sat.

The man smiled. His teeth were very white, but showed no signs of pointed fangs.

He asked, "Do you like my restaurant?"

"Your restaurant?" Jo replied.

"The most recent of very many investments. I come in most nights, to see how it is going. I tend to watch new investments closely until I am certain they are functioning as desired. After that I only need to check once in a while. I'm very pleased with this one, especially as its now afforded me the opportunity to meet the person who destroyed the Countess."

"You're well informed."

"Information is a business of its own. The Countess was also my business."

"You were her backer or something?"

"I had planned to be her executioner, but you saved me the trouble. I'm told you're very efficient. "You did destroy the bloodstone?"

"Yes. I shot it. Had the fragments disposed of over a wide area."

"Excellent."

"So. You're not a vampire, but you know vampires. What exactly are you?"

"I am myself. Perhaps you should order your meal, before I begin to explain."

Carla was back to take the order. Jo ordered. Carla asked the man if he would order, and he declined, but ordered a bottle of wine.

"Presumptuous of me to order wine for both of us, but this is a particularly fine wine, and I believe you will enjoy it," he said.

"You're not eating?"

"An effect of immortality. Food has become boring. I don't need to eat, so I rarely bother. So while we wait for your food to arrive, I must ask, do you know where vampires come from?"

"In my experience, other vampires," Jo said.

"But before that?"

"Before? Was there a before?"

"Oh indeed there was. Are you familiar with the Bible? With the gospels?"

"Sort of."

"Judas Iscariot, was paid thirty pieces of silver to betray Jesus. After the crucifixion, he threw the money away and killed himself in remorse."

"And that relates to vampires, how?"

"That relates to vampires because of what was not included in the Gospels. He was not allowed to die, but left to live to have the opportunity to fully repent."

"What does that mean?"

"You've worked with the undead long enough to know what that means."

"Judas became a vampire?"

"A proto-vampire, a corrupt creature, that walked among humans and created vampires."

"Hanging himself didn't mean he repented?"

"It meant he felt guilt and grief, but no, not fully repentant."

"So you're Judas, repentant?"

The man laughed. "No, but you will find me in that same story. Shortly before he went to his death in Jerusalem, Jesus visited my home. My sisters and I had been among his followers, his closest friends. But this visit was different. I had died three days before. Jesus raised me."

"You're Lazarus?"

"I'm Lazarus."

Jo's meal arrived, along with the wine. Carla poured the wine for both of them, then left.

"And you kill vampires?"

"Not all vampires, like you, I kill those which have actually harmed humans."

"Why?"

"Jesus was my friend. Until Judas betrayed him, I counted him as a friend as well. I am in the world, possibly until the end of time. While I am here, I must do something, so I try to undo the harm that my former friend has done."

"And Judas is still out there somewhere, creating vampires?"

"No. Judas was finally broken and repentant. He lives in a monastery, in an isolated mountain village in Eastern Europe. I visit him sometimes. The harm he did in his bad years, however, lives on."

"And I'm meant to believe all of this?"

"Believe what you will. Read my book, make up your own mind."

"Your book?"

"The fourth gospel, the one tradition attributes to John. The writer only identifies themself as the disciple Jesus loved, and Jesus did indeed love me. He loved me and my sisters. We were family."

"This is all a bit much."

"You live in a world of vampires, zombies, werewolves, and I understand you even have a Yowie on your team, and I'm too much to believe?"

"When you put it that way..."

"All things are possible."

"So, I guess this means that my city has nothing to fear from you?"

"It does not, and neither does that frightened little waitress, but you'll watch me anyway, won't you?"

"Of course."

"I would expect nothing less."

He was utterly beautiful, and charming, and he told a good story, but Jo had no idea whether or not to believe him. After all the Countess had also been beautiful and charming, and wasn't the Devil supposed to have those attributes as well? Whether he was what he said he was or not, Jo would definitely watch him, with the same tenacity as she watched all the other beings in the city.

In a sense Carla had been right, the city was dangerous, particularly at night. Jo was determined to make it less dangerous.

Descendant

"I've heard the Judas story before," Agent Marissa Tyler said. "The whole thing about how Judas was the first vampire, which is why vampires can't cope with silver or crosses, and can be killed with a wooden stake, like the wood from the cross."

"I've heard it before, too. I thought it was from a novel or something, rather than tradition, but I could be wrong," Senior Agent Jo Burns answered. "It's not a new idea. I don't know if I believe it. I also don't know whether or not to believe the rest of his story."

"The whole being Lazarus, the immortal vampire killer?"

"Yeah, that bit."

"I guess that's why you've got us following him around the clock. He knows we're watching him, you know."

"Of course he does. He knew who we were in the restaurant. He knew me by name, and he knew who the rest of the team were, as well. He'd researched us very well. That doesn't mean he's who he says he is. It just means he's thorough. If he came to town to kill the Countess, and found we'd already done that, why did he stay? He not only stayed, but invested in a new restaurant. Did you find out if he did invest in the restaurant? Was that much true?"

"Well that tracks. J. M. Lazarus owns that restaurant, and twenty others in cities around the world. He also owns multiple businesses with serious environmental and social credentials and donates massive amounts to charity each year. He even owns an aid agency that seems to be funded by his businesses. It's all under the umbrella of Lazarus Corp. He's loaded, but on paper he seems like a unicorn, a truly good multi-millionaire. How do all these immortals get so rich, anyway? The Countess had a ton invested."

"I guess if you're around for a thousand or two thousand years and haven't made any money, you're probably not trying. What kind of charities?"

"Schools in third world countries, health, housing, anti-poverty."

"Give your money to the poor."

"Sorry?"

"Back to the Gospels, Jesus telling his followers to give their money to the poor."

"Well he doesn't give everything to the poor, but he probably gives away half his income, which is better than most of the rich people out there. Doesn't claim it as a tax deduction, either. He maximises his tax, in every jurisdiction he has businesses in, instead of minimising it."

"So giving away half his income, and not minimising his taxes, he's keeping what a third of his income? A quarter of it?"

"Given where he has businesses, maybe even less. Doesn't make him poor by any stretch of the imagination, though."

"Well, I'm off to relieve Scott, following our person of interest."

Jo didn't bother hiding that she was following Lazarus. He obviously knew he was being watched, so there was no point.

The waitress, Carla Johanson was leaving work. Lazarus left at the same time. He did not appear to be following the girl, but was walking the same way. They were both going toward Central Station, so it was possible that it was just coincidence. When the girl picked up her pace, Lazarus hung back, apparently realising he was scaring her, and trying not to.

Then it happened. Out of a shadow, a vampire leapt and grabbed the girl.

By the time Jo had pulled out her miniature crossbow, Lazarus had already pulled the fang away, and staked him through the heart.

The fang, seemed to catch fire before disintegrating, a thing Jo had never seen happen.

Lazarus looked back at her, and said: "Wood from the original cross is far more effective than stakes made from any other timber."

He reached out and helped Carla to her feet. Then he said to Jo, "Before I died, I had a wife and a child. While I have been hunting vampires for two thousand years, they have hunted my children and their children. Vampires couldn't kill me, so they killed any heritage I left. Young Carla is the last of my descendants. Her father was killed by a vampire two years ago. That's why she went to you when she realised I was no longer human. I knew she'd gone to you, because I have been following her for weeks. I invested in the restaurant, specifically to give her a job, where I could continue to watch over her."

"So you're staying in Brisbane?"

"I am. And, as I have previously assured you, I am no threat to anyone, except vampires who want to harm humans, particularly vampires who want to harm this one, specific, human."

"Fair enough. Carla, how are you now?"

Carla answered, "Confused, frightened, and curious. I think there's a story here that I need to hear."

Jo said, "There's definitely a story you need to hear, although I'm still not sure I believe it. I do believe my team could move on to other things, now, though."

Lazarus offered her his hand to shake, and Jo left them, walking towards the station together.

Blood

Pathologist Helen Thompson carefully compared the surveillance photos to a set of vampire teeth she kept in her office.

Senior Agent Jo Burns said, "Everything about this guy says he's a fang, except actual fangs."

Helen answered, "None of these photos show his teeth enough for a proper comparison. Anyway, I heard you pulled his surveillance, that you accepted his story."

Jo smiled. "I pulled *our* surveillance. He's researched us, knows us too well. I got David to assign plain clothes police to watch him instead. They don't know why they're following him, just that David needs full reports, so I get full reports."

"So you didn't believe Lazarus' story?"

"Do you? It's a bit out there, even for what we deal with. And the fang he killed caught fire and just burned up. I haven't seen that before. I couldn't tell if it was ancient one, but I didn't see a bloodstone. It was either young, or Lazarus palmed the stone. I don't see why a young vampire would know about this apparently ancient feud. All of which makes me very suspicious. So, is it possible for a vampire to get rid of or somehow disguise his fangs?"

"I suppose he could file them down. It would be a difficult job, and it might have to be repeated regularly. I don't know if they regrow. Vampires recover from any injury, and this would be a kind of injury. It would also be possible that this is a new kind of vampire we haven't encountered before, or an older type, even more ancient than the oldest we've known."

"It would be nice to believe him, believe he's not here with any ill intent, but I made the mistake of believing the Countess. Normally, the creatures we deal with don't draw attention to themselves. Lazarus made sure that girl, Carla, knew he wasn't human. He knew she would seek help. The Countess was the only other creature who went out of their way to get in contact."

"You think he has some hidden agenda?"

"I think it's a distinct possibility."

They were interrupted by Jo's mobile phone ringing. When Jo answered, Inspector David Webber said, "We've got something."

Jo, along with agents Kate Murdoch and Scott Cooper, arrived at the scene moments after David.

He was already with two plain clothes officers. They were on the front steps of a church.

Carla, the waitress Lazarus had been interested in, was lying on the steps of the church. Her neck was bleeding and she was shaking, pale and apparently in shock.

"Ambulance is coming," David said.

Jo replied, "No ambulance, they'll ask too many questions, and won't be able to help. We need Helen. Did Lazarus do this? The other target?"

One of the plain clothes officers said, "No, it was someone else. The other target chased the offender off. We don't know where either of them are now."

Jo looked at the girl's neck. The fangs hadn't cut deep. The fang hadn't had the opportunity to drain her blood. Of course, death from exsanguination wasn't necessarily the worst possible effect of a vampire bite.

"There's a good chance she's infected. Hopefully Helen will be able to do something to stop the bite taking effect. It must have been an ancient one to attack in daylight, and on the church steps."

Scott had been on the phone. He said, "Helen says keep her warm, and she's on her way. She'll bring blood to start a transfusion in the car."

Jo's phone rang. "Agent Burns," a familiar voice said. "I was unable to catch the vampire that attacked Carla. I presume the police officers you had following us have called you in time. Your pathologist will be bringing O positive blood, as it is safe to transfuse to most people. In fact Carla is O positive, so it will be perfect for her. Carla will need a complete transfusion, draining all of her own blood and replacing it within the next six hours, if she is to survive. That transfusion will be a great trauma on her human body. I suggest adding a small amount of my blood to the transfusion. Tell me where to meet you to take it. I know your pathologist will want to examine my blood and attempt to ascertain if it can harm Carla. It cannot harm her, but you will want to be as certain as you can. I know you will not want to invite me into your office, as you still suspect I may be a vampire, and an invitation to a vampire is a permanent invitation. Please come to my house. The police officers who have been following me have my address."

Helen arrived with Andrew Harrison. Andrew picked Carla up easily and placed her gently in the back of Helen's car. Then he held a blood bag for Helen, and she began the transfusion.

Scott drove Helen's car with Andrew and Carla in the back to the HDU office. Then Andrew carried the unconscious girl to the pathology unit, while Scott carried the blood bag, held high.

Jo, and Kate accompanied Helen to Lazarus' house.

He invited them in and offered his arm to Helen to take three vials of blood, one for testing, and two to add to Carla's transfusions if it looked safe.

He told them that should they want more of his blood to have some stored for future cases of vampire attack, he would comply, once Carla was well again.

They thanked him and left, Jo realising that she had not left anyone watching Lazarus, but anxious to save Carla.

At the HDU offices, Helen changed Carla's blood bag over to a new one, telling Andrew he would be responsible for the next one.

Then she began a venesection, to slowly drain Carla's own blood.

"Doesn't the new blood mix with the old?" Jo asked.

"Yes," Helen said, "but the new blood will dilute what's circulating. Do me a favour and watch that this keeps flowing slowly like this. If it stops, of speeds up, call me. I'm going to look at Lazarus' blood sample and see what's what."

Helen spent an hour or more studying the blood. In that time Andrew changed over a new blood bag, and Jo emptied and replaced the small steel jug that was receiving the blood from the venesection.

Helen came back. "I officially don't know," she said. "It's not vampire, but it's not human either, and I don't know what it will do."

On the gurney, Carla's body began to shake and jerk.

"Damn, she's seizing," Helen said. "It's not working. Do we take the risk?"

"Do it," Jo said.

Helen injected a vial of Lazarus' blood into the plastic tube Carla was receiving the infusion through.

The seizure stopped immediately. Colour returned to Carla's pallid face, and her body warmed.

The blood from the venesection stopped flowing, and the needle popped out, leaving no mark where it had been. The transfusion needle also popped out of her arm, as if it had been sprung free with rubber band under tension. That also left no mark. Helen looked at Carla's neck, and the fang marks were gone.

Carla sat up and asked where she was.

Jo explained the situation as simply as possible.

Helen asked how she was, and checked her vital signs.

"Can I go now?" Carla asked.

Helen sounded surprised as she answered, "You look perfectly fine. There's no sign of anything wrong, but given what you've just been through, I'd like to keep you here under observation for a while."

Carla asked, "Can I please talk to Lazarus?"

Jo tried to call back the number Lazarus had called her on earlier. There was no answer.

She sent Kate and Scott to go and see him.

They soon reported in that, in the three hours since Helen had taken his blood, he had gone. His house was completely empty.

"He's must have better removalists than I've ever used," Jo said. "I've never been able to move house that fast. Check his restaurant."

A short while later, the two agents would report back that the restaurant was also empty, and had a notice on the door saying it was closed permanently.

Jo broke the news of Lazarus' leaving to Carla.

Then she told Helen to perform every test she possibly could on that last vial of Lazarus' blood. She suspected they had been manipulated into injecting it into Carla, and she wanted to know why.

Remembering the Future

Senior Agent Jo Burns had expected to hear from Carla again. She hadn't expected the nature of the call she'd receive.

"Two vampires are going to try to kill me tonight. They can't harm me, but if you don't manage to stop them tonight, they'll go on to kill dozens of humans before you do."

Picking off two vampires with miniature crossbows with wooden bolts, proved to be easy for Jo and Agent Marissa Tyler, who were waiting for the two vampires who were stalking Carla as she walked home that night.

They were old vampires, and turned to dust, leaving bloodstones, which Jo despatched in what had become her usual fashion.

Jo turned to Carla and said, "Now I want to know…"

"How I knew they were coming for me and what they'd do after? Yes, I know you do. It began with that blood transfusion, with the Lazarus blood added. You were worried about not knowing the effect it would have."

"Yes, we did…"

"You had Dr Thompson do every test she could, and couldn't find out what was so special about it. At first, I didn't know either, but then I started having regular feelings of deja vu."

"Deja vu?"

"Yes, deja vu. I had a sense of having done things before. Your phone's about to ring. The mechanic says your car's going to take a bit longer, and it will cost an extra thousand dollars."

At that moment Jo's phone rang. It was indeed the mechanic, to tell her that the repairs that were being done would take an extra day and would cost about a thousand dollars more.

"How did you?"

"How did I know? Well after a couple of days, with increasingly frequent bouts of deja vu, I began having, well, they felt like memories, but of things that hadn't happened yet. It was as if I'd lived everything before and knew what would happen next.At first I noticed simple things, like I was reading a book and remembered a typo on the next page, 'dug' was written as 'dog'. When I got to it, there it was, exactly as I remembered it."

"So you can tell the future?"

"And then I wanted to know if I could change the things I remembered. I remembered a woman and a little girl being hit by a car, and when I saw them about to cross the road, I stopped them and asked for directions. The car sped past exactly as I remembered it, but the girl and her mother were safe on the footpath because I'd changed what had happened. So things don't have to be exactly as I remember them. I can change them. So to answer your question, it can't be telling the future if it can be changed, because that wouldn't be the future, would it?"

"I haven't really thought about..."

"No, you haven't thought about it because you haven't heard about it before now, but I've thought about it. I think it might be something to do with parallel universes or something. I think I'm somehow seeing what another me sees in another universe, before it happens in this one, and I can change it."

"You think that's a more logical explanation that foreseeing the future? Not just that if you know the future you can change it?"

"I knew you were going to say that, but I think my theory is probably more correct, because it feels more like a memory."

146

"So you foresaw these vampires were going to kill multiple other people."

"Yes, and it was going to take you weeks to catch them. But I knew they would be here tonight for an attempt on me. So I decided to call you tonight to stop them, and prevent all of those deaths."

"Which I appreciate, but..."

"But now you don't know for sure that what I remembered happening was really going to happen. And you can't know. And I can't know, except that I know that if I remember a thing happening and I don't do anything to change it, it happens."

"You know you..."

"Were a lot less talkative before I had the Lazarus blood, yes."

"Ah yes."

"I know. I guess I'm more confident now. I always thought I never really knew what was going on in the world around me. Now I know too much of what's going on. And I have money to do anything I ever want. That's another thing that's different. I've been getting payments in my bank account from Lazarus Corporation every month. I haven't heard from Lazarus, and he doesn't seem to have of his businesses left in Brisbane, they all just closed. But he's sending me money. So I can remember things that haven't happened yet, and I'm rich. And to answer your next question, I can only remember a couple of weeks ahead so far, but it's been getting longer, and I don't know how far ahead it will end up being. And no, I don't know if I'm immortal like Lazarus or not. I know the vampires couldn't harm me. Nothing can penetrate my skin if I don't want it to. But yes, I will let Dr Thompson take blood, skin and hair samples when she asks next week, so she can study further. You're going to go and process all of this information, and when I come in for my samples, you're going to offer me a job, that I don't want or need. So I'll just make it easy now and tell you I'm available as a consultant when you need one, and I'll call you if I remember anything you need to know."

"OK."

"Well, good night now. You and Agent Tyler are going to have a long talk about me in the car on the way back to your office."

Jo and Marissa left, and they did indeed, have a long talk about Carla on the way back to the office.

Acceleration

Senior Agent Jo Burns was in the lab with Pathologist Helen Thompson.

"I don't know what to make of it," Helen said. "Carla's blood looks similar to Lazarus' blood, but not quite the same."

"What's the difference? Still part human?"

"You mean, like a chimera? No, it's more a like degraded version of Lazarus' sample. Take a look."

Helen put two slides on an electronic microscope and showed Jo the image on a monitor.

She said, "The slide on the left is the Lazarus sample, and the one on the right is Carla's. The cells look similar, but the edges of Carla's are less defined."

"So that means?"

"It's breaking down, or aging? I think. I've never dealt with anything like this before."

"That doesn't sound good."

"No, it doesn't. Skin and hair samples were odd too. They're not quite human, again, the cells seem to break down quickly. I can show you the slides if you like."

"Showing me is probably not going to help me any more than you telling me. Is she dying? Did we save her only to have her die anyway?"

"I honestly don't know. The other weird thing was the way she was behaving."

"Talking at triple speed?"

"Not only that, but she carried the whole conversation. She said what I was going to say, then responded with a huge amount of information, then continued with what I was going to say next. It was exhausting."

"She was like that when Marissa and I saw her. I would start a sentence, and she'd finish it for me, and continue on with her response. I barely got to say a word."

"I didn't get to say a single word. It was just a wall of her speech, and it got faster as she talked. She started out sounding like she was on speed, and it just ramped up from there."

Jo thought a moment, "She was a bit like that with me. It sounds like it's getting more extreme? Dare I say worse?"

"Like she's accelerating."

"She told me her 'remembering the future' thing was letting her see further and further ahead. Could this be part of it?"

"You think they teach foretelling the future at med school?"

"Didn't fortune tellers use entrails? There's a bit of crossover there."

"I was away that week, missed the divining from entrails class."

"Pity, it might have been useful. Medical school probably prepared you for your job as well as the police academy prepared me for mine."

"So do we call Carla and tell her the results?"

"She would've already known last week."

Helen said, "We did this to her, whatever 'this' is."

Jo replied, "We were out of options. It was either try this, or let her die."

"I wonder if whatever 'this' is will turn out to be better. Have you tracked down Lazarus?"

"Not him. But we've followed the money Carla's been receiving from him to a bank in the Cayman Islands. I'd consider sending someone if there was even the slightest chance of getting information, but tax shelters never cooperate. So still no Lazarus and we still don't know his motivation.

"Have you thought that, if he had this foresight or whatever it is that Carla now has, he would have known about the attack on Carla beforehand? He should have been able to prevent it, or get you to prevent it?"

"That had crossed my mind. It would mean he intended all along to have us inject Carla with his blood."

"That's what I was thinking. That bothers me."

"Me too. It bothers me a lot."

Metamorphosis

Senior Agent Jo Burns received a text from Carla, the waitress who, after a vampire attack, had been administered blood from the immortal being known as Lazarus.

The text said: "Lazarus will be at my house on Tuesday at 1pm. We will answer all your questions then. Please bring Dr Thompson, as she will want to take more samples."

Jo passed the message on to HDU pathologist Helen Thompson, who absolutely did want to be there.

When they arrived, they were surprised to see the change in Carla.

She was not the shy waitress they had first met, nor was she the girl who talked constantly at high speed they'd seen more recently. Now she carried herself with the same air of dignity and grace that Lazarus himself did. She seemed to glow, to even radiate light. She had a strange red glow around the iris of her eyes, which almost looked like flames.

Carla smiled and graciously welcomed them, with the same easy elegant charm she had first noticed in Lazarus when she'd met him at the restaurant where Carla had worked.

Lazarus himself greeted them warmly. "I know you have many questions, Agent Burns, which I will answer, and Dr Thompson wants to take more samples from both of us, and we would not stand in the way of science.

Jo said, "Carla, you look different."

Carla smiled and said, "Just a bit."

Lazarus said, "You were concerned for Carla's well-being when you saw her last, were you not? A caterpillar doesn't enter the cocoon and immediately become a butterfly. It's a process. Metamorphosis takes time. You saw her half way through her transformation. As you can see now, it's almost complete. A little while and she have full control of the glow."

"Metamorphosis? So she's changing into?"

"Into what I am. Do we have a name? We've called ourselves the Lazarai. When I said Carla was the last of my descendants, that was a white lie. She was the next I that I foresaw would be attacked by vampires. Vampire venom is the catalyst that allows the change, along with an injection of my blood."

"Why did you involve us in this? It seems you've done this before, so you didn't need our help."

Lazarus smiled broadly. "Because, my dear Agent Burns, you are too good at your job. I saw that you would be there to interrupt the vampire attack and try to save Carla. So I arranged it so we would meet ahead of time, and I would give you an explanation for my interest in Carla, so you wouldn't be suspicious of my attempt to help her. I involved you, because you were going to involve yourself."

"And how much of the original story you told me was true?"

"Practically all of it. The part which was untrue was that Carla was my only descendant. I have many. Quite a number of them are now immortals. Whenever I see that one of my descendants will be attacked by a vampire I ensure I am on hand to inject them with my blood, to save them, and to transform them."

"So the whole vampires attacking your family was true?"

"There are many branches to my family tree, as you would imagine over two thousand years. One of those branches has specialised in hunting vampires. They call themselves by the name of Van Helsing, after one o the more famous members of their clan."

"And yet you need vampires to bite your family members, so you can do this transformation?"

"It's more that a vampire bite creates a necessity. That necessity has a side-effect. Much better to be Lazarai than a vampire."

"But you only do this for your own descendants?"

"I've only ever tried it on my own descendants. I don't know what it would do to others. Perhaps Dr Thompson's research will answer that. Perhaps she will use my blood to develop a vampire anti-venom that does not have side effects. I know she will try. I can't see far enough ahead to know if she will succeed. I will give you a way to contact me, should you need me to return to give more blood for that purpose."

"Apart from vampire hunting, what do Lazarai do with their immortality?"

"Each of us is free to do as they choose, but most of us work for humanitarian causes. We have our own aid agency. Being immortal allows us to safely go into areas of rampant disease, war, disaster. Being our own agency, we're able to disguise that our people live so much longer than people really should. And we have our own source of income, so we're not tied to funding from governments or private donations. It's one of the larger aid agencies, you have heard of it, but I'm not going to tell you which it is."

"The money comes from Lazarus Corp? But where does its money come from? Are your businesses really enough to support it?"

"Oh Agent Burns, you've already worked that out, haven't you?"

"A group of people who can see the future. I imagine a strategic gambling win here or there?"

"Each of us wins a large amount every decade or so, not often enough to attract attention. The winnings are paid into the Lazarus Corp account, and all of us are paid a stipend each month, and all of our work is funded through it as well.

We don't choose the tax haven to avoid paying our share of taxes, but to avoid questions being asked."

"So you have immortality, unlimited money, and you spend it it humanitarian work?"

"I told you my story already. What else did you expect? I do what my mentor taught me. I mentor my people to do the same. Not all of them choose to go into the family business, but many do."

"And this family business is humanitarian aid and vampire killing?"

"We also have an environmental protection branch."

"So what happens with Carla, when her metamorphosis is complete?"

"That's up to Carla herself."

Carla said, "I'll go out to work in crisis areas with the agency. I'll be a nurse's assistant at first, but I'll study on line and eventually become a frontline nurse. If it turns out I don't like nursing, I can train for something else. I have all the time in the world."

Van Helsing

A package had arrived for Pathologist Helen Thompson.

"More Lazarus blood?" Senior Agent Jo Burns asked.

Helen replied, "Six vials. The great thing about a research subject who can see the future is that whenever I'm running low, he sends more."

"Shouldn't that have cold packs or something to preserve it?"

"No need. This stuff doesn't coagulate, doesn't deteriorate. It's practically indestructible."

"Where is Lazarus now?"

Helen looked at the sender's address on the package: "Sierra Leone. I heard there's an Ebola outbreak there."

"Sounds like fun. I wonder if Carla's there too."

"Possibly. I expect they need lots of nurses, and indestructible nurses are hard to come by.."

Later in the day, Jo received a call.

The caller said, "Hi Jo, I'm Kevin Burns from the Van Helsing clan of the Lazarai. Lazarus has left a standing order that if we're ever hunting in Brisbane, we should report to you. Want to join us for a coffee?"

Jo agreed to meet at a coffee shop near the Roma Street Police Station.

Kevin Burns, who said he usually went by "Kev", and his hunting partner Andrea Domichi, explained to her that they were hunting a fifteen hundred year old vampire, they'd tracked from Eastern Europe, west to England, then to Australia. He had always been several steps ahead of them.

"Jo, I'm going to ask you not to get involved in our hunt. We've both seen you getting bitten, so we want you to stay away from it," Kev said.

"Not getting involved is difficult for me," Jo answered. "But if you can tell me how I end up getting bitten, perhaps I can avoid that specific thing."

"If you're going to get involved, and you are bitten, you know we have to kill you. We don't have Lazarus here to give you his blood in time to save you."

"My pathologist has plenty of Lazarus' blood. But it wouldn't help me she hasn't found a cure with it yet, and the actual blood only works on his descendants."

Kev looked surprised. He said, "You don't know?"

"Know what."

Kev took out his phone, and pulled up a large diagram of a family tree. "This is you here. If I click on your name, the red line appears and you can trace back, your father, grand father, great-great grandfather, great-great-great grandmother, just follow back you'll see."

Jo followed the line back until she got to the surname Van Helsing, and didn't bother going back any further.

Kev said, "Now go back to your great-great grandfather William, or as we called him, Billy. You see his brother Kevin listed? With the name in yellow instead of black? That's me I'm your great-great-great uncle. I'll send you the link to the family tree if you like. If we become Lazarai, the name gets changed to yellow."

Jo was quiet, trying to absorb the information. Then she asked, "So how did you become Lazarai?"

"World War One. I was in a prisoner of war camp, and attacked by a vampire. At the same time, Lazarus was demanding admission as a Red Cross inspector, to inspect the prisoners' living conditions. The Red Cross rarely got to inspect anything, no matter how much they demanded, but Lazarus can charm anyone, and they let him and an assistant in. While doing their inspection, the assistant killed the vampire, and Lazarus gave me his blood. The guards didn't notice or suspect anything. I think Lazarus may have given someone a substantial bribe to not notice. After the war, he found me and explained everything. His Red Cross days were when he learned everything he needed to set up his own aid agency."

Jo said, "How about you, Andrea? How did you become Lazarai?"

Andrea answered, "I was on my college campus, when Lazarus started hanging out at the Student Union building, running some kind of educational campaign about safety on campus. Every time I went in there, he warned me about the dangers of walking home alone after classes at night. He offered me money to get a taxi. I was more worried about taking money from a stranger than the walk home at night, especially since he seemed to be more concerned about me than other women. So, I continued walking home at night, not knowing he was following me. When the vampire attacked, he was there to fight it off, but I still had a graze from one of its fangs. So Lazarus gave me a choice, I could become a vampire and someone would have to kill me, or he could turn me into an immortal like him. I chose immortality."

Kev said, "So, if you do get involved in this, and you do get bitten, what do you choose? Since we might not be able to ask you at the time?"

Jo thought a while before answering, "I absolutely don't want to be a vampire, even if you would let me, so I'll take the blood over death. But fill me in on what you've seen happening, and maybe we can avoid the choice all together."

So they told her how they had seen themselves waiting outside the vampire's hotel and following him until he reached a secluded area, then all three would attack. Jo would use her miniature crossbow, which would hit the vampire, but miss his heart. The enraged vampire would attack her, while the others would grab him, hold him down and stake him.

"So all we have to do is change the plan. We skip the crossbow. You two tackle him and hold him down, and I'll do the staking."

Kev said, "I'd feel better about it if you weren't there at all."

Jo said, "And I feel better being part of every anti-supernatural monster action that happens in this city."

Kev reluctantly agreed, then looked to the empty seat beside Jo and said, "Little Katie, will you please help us try to keep your stubborn mother safe?"

Jo was stunned. She'd often felt Katie close by, often heard her, or seen her in dreams, but had never expected anyone else to notice the ghost child.

Jo asked, hesitantly, "You can see her?"

Kev turned his attention back to her, "Sorry," he said. "I keep forgetting that humans usually can't see ghosts."

Jo called Helen, and told her about the vampire hunt, the prediction, and about the issue and the plan to deal with it if things went wrong.

Helen tried to talk her into sitting this one out, but her pleas fell on deaf ears.

As the vampire was an old one, he was able to move freely in sunlight.

Jo, Andrea and Kev went straight from the coffee shop to wait across the road from the vampire's hotel. The Lazarai's foresight saved a lot of time in researching and tracking.

Kev gave Jo a bag to carry. It contained a hammer and wooden stakes. He told her that she was to stay well out of the vampire's reach until he and Andrea had it pinned down.

Jo held back and followed Kev and Andrea from a distance, as they stalked the vampire. They followed it to a back alley, behind a row of restaurants. There, the vampire stood still, and blended into the shadows, presumably waiting to hunt some restaurant worker when they came outside to put rubbish in the bins, or have a smoke break.

Then Kev and Andrea leapt into action, they took the vampire down with a practiced precision, and held him.

Jo approached, placed the stake on the vampire's chest, and lifted the hammer.

The vampire jerked, pulling itself from its captors' grasp momentarily. They immediately re-secured their hold, and each pushed a shoulder down, his head seemed to be also pulled down by some invisible force.(Jo had a fleeting thought of Katie.) In the struggle, a fang grazed Jo's hand.

Jo hammered the stake home. The ancient vampire turned to dust. Kevin crushed the bloodstone under the heel of his boot.

Then, they took Jo straight to the HDU. She was drifting out of consciousness, as they arrived in Helen's lab. With little time left, Helen administered the injection.

Over the next few days, Helen insisted Jo was not to leave the lab, and someone was always to be with her.

As her mind raced, and a fever raged, every part of her body changed, at an ever-increasing rate. When she spoke, her speech was much faster than normal. She began having flashes of what felt like memories, of things that hadn't happened yet.

For a week, Jo's HDU team mates, Kev, Andrea, and her ex-husband Police Inspector David Webber, all took turns at keeping her company.

For the whole time, a little girl in a Red Riding Hood costume, invisible to humans, stayed right beside her.

When Jo reached the stage where her blood cells looked like the Lazarus cells, her skin glowed, and her eyes had a ring of fire around the pupil, Helen declared her well enough to leave the lab.

Kev asked her, "What are you going to do now? Are you going to join the family business? Hunt vampires with us? Help in disaster areas with Lazarus? Something entirely different?"

Jo said, "First, I'm taking a week off to spend with my daughter, since I've only seen her in dreams for the past few years. Otherwise, I'm going to stay right where I am, and keep doing my job."

"That's fine for the next twenty-five years or so, but if you're outside the family business, you will need to change your identity, and move on, or people will notice."

Jo smiled, "But I don't exist, and I'm working for an organisation that doesn't exist. Being an immortal, immune to vampires, who has to concentrate to allow even the minor injury of having a needle for a blood test, will just make me even better at my job."

The day after Kev and Andrea caught a flight to Luxembourg, on the hunt for another ancient vampire, Jo discovered her first monthly stipend payment from Lazarus Corp was in her bank account. She hadn't provided her bank details to anyone, but somehow they knew. Of course, they knew. Jo also received an email with instructions on how to deposit a once-a-decade gambling win into the Lazarus Corp account to continue funding the Lazarai, and the family business.

They were efficient. She had to give them credit for that.

Bad Doggy

Senior Agent Jo Burns hadn't taken leave in the three years since she began at the Human Defence Unit.

When she decided to take all of her annual leave at once, she had twelve weeks owing.

Jo still had two weeks of leave left, as she sat on quiet beach, near the sandcastle she'd built, under direction from a small girl in a Red Riding Hood costume. A small girl who did not cast a shadow.

The ghost of her daughter Katie asked, "Is it far enough from the water, Mummy? Will it still be here tomorrow?"

"I don't know," Jo answered. "I'm not sure how high the tide comes up."

"If it is still here, can we make it bigger?"

"Of course we can. Anything you want. But didn't you want to go to a theme park tomorrow?"

"Oh yes. The one with the polar bears! Or the one with the tigers! No polar bears."

"We've still got two weeks. We can see both. Polar bears tomorrow and Tigers next week, how about that?"

"Yes!" The little girl jumped up and down in excitement, leaving no marks on the sand at all.

It was strange, but for three years, Jo had only seen her murdered daughter in dreams, so she was happy to have Katie back in any way.

Suddenly, Jo had a flash of what felt like a memory, but what she knew was the future.

She saw her second-in-charge Agent Marissa Tyler walking, unsuspecting into a small shop. It looked like it could be a neighbourhood fish and chip shop, the type that had a small range of grocery items as well.

There were two small tables, each with two chairs, where customers could wait for their order, or eat in. There was a fridge of soft drinks, and a freezer of ice blocks. There was a rack with loaves of bread, and shelves of lollies, potato chips, and all of the general small grocery items such shops had.

Marissa walked in, chose a soft drink and took it to the counter, where she ordered her meal and paid. As she turned to sit at a table and wait for her meal to be cooked, a werewolf smashed through the window and attacked her.

The premonition ended at that point. Jo didn't know when it would happen, or exactly where. She didn't know how to avoid it.

She rang Marissa and told her everything she'd seen. She described the shop in detail.

"That sounds like the fish and chip shop just near my place," Marissa said. "I guess we watch it every full moon until the werewolf turns up. Thanks for the warning. Enjoy the rest of your holiday."

Jo pressed "end call" and got up from the sand, picking up the rug she had been sitting on.

"Bad doggy," Katie said.

"Did you see that as well?" Jo asked.

"The bad doggy wants to hurt your friend. He watches her."

"You mean when he's not a wolf, when he's human?"

"He's very bad. Hurting people is bad."

"Hurting people is very bad. But if he's watching her when he's not a wolf, he's even more dangerous."

"We have to go home, don't we, Mummy?"

Jo sighed. "Yes, I'm afraid we do. First I have to call Marissa again."

163

Jo made the call, explaining that Katie had extra information, and that Marissa had a stalker.

"I'm packing up now. I can be in the office in a couple of hours," Jo said.

"You don't have to come back. We can handle it."

"I'm not leaving you in danger. I'll be at the office in a couple of hours."

"What about your time with Katie?"

"She's coming too."

Jo returned to the hotel and packed her bag, and checked out.

The highway was packed, all four lanes full of cars driving from the Gold Coast to Brisbane.

"Go fast, Mummy," Katie said.

"Have you seen something?"

"Go fast. Don't let the bad doggy hurt your friend."

Jo pulled the flashing blue light from the glove box, put it on the dash board and hit the siren. It was something she hadn't done in the past three years, not since her time as a police officer, a time that ended with Katie's murder.

As other drivers tried to get out of her way, Jo wove between between lanes, choosing the fastest, clearest path she could see.

"What are you seeing, Katie?"

"Your friend is drinking coffee, and the doggy is watching her."

"In the office?"

"No, Mummy, where you go for coffee at lunch time."

"The coffee shop? Near the police station?"

"Yes Mummy."

Jo suddenly saw it. Marissa was sitting at a table, drinking a coffee. A short man, with a shaggy brown beard was sitting at another table, ostensibly drinking coffee, but really just staring at the back of Marissa's head.

"Siri, call Marissa," Jo commanded her phone. As the phone connected, Jo could see Marissa picking up the phone.

"Bearded guy, behind you, watching you. He's your stalker wolf."

Marissa jumped up and turned, but the man was already gone. He'd left while Jo and Marissa were on the phone.

"I'm still an hour out. Go back to the office. Stay there," Jo said.

Marissa looked around. The coffee shop was a small one, with no security cameras. She looked around the street outside, and didn't see any bearded men.

She took her coffee back to the office.

There she told Agent Kate Murdoch and Pathologist Helen Thompson about her calls from Jo.

"A pity she doesn't have control of her premonitions," Helen said. "It seemed the older Lazarai had some control of it, or have more information from it."

"We don't exactly know how that all works," Kate said. "We do know when the next full moon is, though, and its two days away. So if you're going to be attacked then, you can't be alone that night. I can't be with you, of course, but Scot and Elizabeth, or Andrew or the Yowie could. Maybe you could just spend the night here."

"No," Marissa said, "that's the one time we know where he will be If he's dangerous, we have to catch him. I have to be bait."

"Probably smart, but I don't like the idea at all," Jo said, as she entered the room.

"Well, boss, you'd better make sure he doesn't actually get me. We already have one agent who can't work on the full moon, we don't need another."

"Maybe we don't have to wait," Kate said. "You know my senses are heightened getting close to the full moon. We know he was at the coffee shop in the past couple of hours. Maybe I can track him. If he didn't get in a car or on a train or a bus."

"Pretty unlikely in the city, but we should give it a go," Jo said. "Silver bullets everyone."

Jo, Kate and Marissa loaded their weapons.

Kate stood in the doorway of the coffee shop and inhaled deeply.

"Yep, got him, only one wolf other than me has been here. This way."

She turned and walked down the street.

"Mummy, he's a tricky doggy," Katie said.

Jo had a sudden flash of the man with the shaggy beard. He was coming up behind them.

"Behind us," Jo said.

They all turned, and walked back the way they'd come.

The man was standing in front of the police station.

Jo approached him, hand close to her gun.

"You've been following my friend," she said.

"She's beautiful. I'm in love with her," he answered.

"Kind of creepy, just following her."

"I was trying to build up the nerve to talk to her."

"Talk to her? Not to attack her?"

"No. I wouldn't do that."

"But you would. On the full moon, when you don't know what you're doing, and you're obsessing over her."

"When I don't know what I'm doing?"

"You lose time don't you? About once a month?"

"How do you know that?"

"Oh, I think I know a lot about you that you don't know yourself. Come into my office. We have a lot to talk about."

It took hours before Jo was able to get through to the man that he was, in fact, a werewolf, and that was the reason he lost time on the night of the full moon.

Then she gave him the standard options: stay in the HDU cells on the full moon, or find his own way to secure himself.

"So here's the rules," Jo said, finally, "You do whatever you have, to avoid being a threat to humans. I can put you in contact with the Werewolf Watch, which is like a neighbourhood watch, but also a support group for local wolves. They'll help you adapt to the life you have now. If you pose any threats to humans, I will kill you, I will kill you to defend the human community. If you don't leave my friend alone, I will kill you for being a creep. Get out of my office, and I don't want to see you again, unless you actually need to report a threat to me."

After he left, Jo asked Katie, "What do you think? Did I scare him enough?"

"He's going to be a good doggy," Katie said.

"Glad to hear it."

Mrs X

Senior Agent Jo Burns was sitting at the desk in her office, doing the paperwork that even non-existent organisations needed.

In a chair on the other side of the desk sat a small girl in a Red Riding Hood costume, swinging her feet while she waited.

The HDU's police liaison, Inspector David Webber, knocked on the door and entered.

The girl said, "Hello Daddy."

Jo looked up. "Hi David. Katie says hello." Jo pointed to where Katie sat.

David looked toward the empty chair, "Hi Katie. I miss you so much."

Katie skipped over to him and hugged him.

David felt suddenly cold.

"She's hugging you," Jo said.

"I've felt that before. I didn't know what it was."

"Me, too. It's weird seeing her now. So what brings you down to the dungeon?"

David put a photo on the desk in front of Jo. It showed a torso back, with white clothes pushed aside, and the words "Jo Burns will die" carved on it.

"This was a psych nurse. A young man who was looking after a high security patient known by the pseudonym Mrs X."

Jo sighed. "She's a very dangerous and skilled practitioner of dark magic. I arrested her husband for serial murder when I was a detective. He died in prison. Then after I started here, she created a zombie and sent him to kill me."

"Zombie? That was Andrew, who helps out in your pathology department?"

"He didn't want to go home to his family after they had already buried him. So he started working here, and let them continue thinking he's dead. How did Mrs X get hold of whatever she used to do this?"

"Believe it or not, she'd been so well behaved, they let her have a plastic knife for her food, instead of whatever they were doing before that."

"That's all she'd need. Well, she's clearly behind on the news if she thinks she can kill me, but we can't let her roam free. She's way too dangerous."

David looked at the photo. "Pretty sure this young nurse and his parents would agree with you. So any premonitions of whatever they are?"

Jo shook her head. "Sorry, I can't control it, yet. Not sure if I ever will be able to. Katie, do you know where the bad lady who wants to hurt me is?"

The ghost child seemed to concentrate. "No Mummy, she's not close."

"Not close," Jo repeated. "Of course, she might also have some way of hiding herself from ghosts or premonitions or whatever."

"Well, the one thing we know she plans to do is to try to kill you. So, I think we should make sure you're always under surveillance."

"That doesn't sound like much fun. I get it. I'm not in any danger, but we do need to catch her, so I guess I'll call the team together and organise this."

Jo called all of her team members, including Andrew and the Yowie, and explained what was happening.

"You haven't seen when she's going to try to attack you?" Marissa asked.

Jo shook her head. She explained that they needed to organise to have team members shadow her whenever she was away from the office.

Kate Murdoch suggested that perhaps Jo could take some time off, leave the office early, spend a lot of time outside. "There's no point in having the perfect bait if she's sitting in a secure area, when she could be dangled out to be hunted," she said.

"Good doggy," Katie said, and skipped over to stand beside Kate.

Kate put a hand on the top of Katie's head. "Not a doggy for two more nights, little one," she said.

"Wait, you can see her too?" David asked.

"Only near the full moon. She hangs out in the cells on the night of the full moon, to keep the 'doggies' company. All the wolves who spend the full moon in our cells know her," Kate said.

"Is anyone else able to see my daughter?" David asked.

The Yowie patted him on the head.

"Actually, that helps us," Agent Marissa Tyler said. "If we have Kate on one team and the Yowie on another, teams can hang back, and Katie can alert us when to move in. You don't need to let her know you're sending us a message, if Katie can do it. If that's OK with Katie."

"I'll help," Katie said.

"She says she's OK with it, "Jo said. "So here's a plan. Three teams: Marissa, and David, if you're with us, stay close enough to see me. Kate, Scott and Elizabeth further back. Yowie and Andrew have to stay out of sight anyway so you're the final reserve. I guess I'm going out for a coffee, to have a walk along the river then go home. Remember, watch out for civilians, so try not to use guns or crossbows if we can avoid them, and Yowie and Andrew, you guys definitely stay out of sight as much as possible."

Jo began her walk, stopping to pick up a coffee, taking her time, watching the area around her closely. She could see Marissa and David about two hundred metres behind her. The others were out of sight.

Jo had a sudden image of the future. Mrs X was hiding between her house and the carport, exactly where Andrew had been made to hide when he'd been forced to attempt to kill her.

Jo waved David and and Marissa over to her, and told them. Then she told Katie, "Go tell everyone what I've just told Marissa and Daddy. Tell them I'm going back to work to get my car from the car park and driving home. Tell all the others, to meet at the car park at work." She could have called them on the mobile, but she wanted to practice the system, which would help them in a situation where they couldn't call.

Katie vanished. Jo, David and Marissa ran back to the office. As the other two teams were closer to the office, they all arrived at the same time.

Jo told the team, "So after our pointless game of follow-the-leader, all we've achieved is to give her time to get into place. Here's the new plan. I will go a little ahead of you all. If she sees all of us arriving she'll run. Park close, but not too close. Sneak through neighbours' yards and over the fence. Don't let her see you coming."

They reorganised. Jo took her own car, the others organising themselves between two other cars.

Jo drove home, with Katie in the passenger seat.

She took her time parking, and getting her handbag out of the car, trying to look as if she didn't suspect anything at all.

Walking from the car to the house, she looked straight ahead, but used her peripheral vision to watch where she knew Mrs X was hiding.

The woman leapt out from her hiding place, stabbing at Jo with a knife. She looked surprised when the knife, would not penetrate Jo's skin.

"Yeah, I've had an upgrade since your last attempt," Jo said, as she grabbed the woman's hand, and twisted. She smelled something, and realised the knife was probably poisoned, as well as being very sharp. Jo was determined that whatever was on the knife, it was not going to harm any of her team.

Mrs X struggled, and Jo grabbed the knife with both hands, knowing neither the blade nor any poison would hurt her.

As Jo pulled the knife from her attacker, the woman was lifted up high into the air. Andrew Harrison had come up behind her and picked her up.

"He's still a bit upset about you turning him into a zombie," Jo said. "I wouldn't do anything to enrage him if I were you."

The woman screamed and twisted out of Andrew's grip.

Other team members had arrived and surrounded her.

"How about just giving up now, and going back to your hospital room?" Jo suggested.

The woman lunged at Jo, trying to grab the knife back from her, but caught the blade.

A sizzling sound came from the hand where she cut it, and smoke poured out from the wound. The woman screamed, as what looked like chemical burns spread from her hand up her arm and then throughout her body.

Eventually, the magic practitioner was just an odiferous, gelatinous, blob, on the lawn.

Jo looked at the team, who were all standing, looking stunned.

"Right," she said. "David, we need your people to block off the street and make sure no-one comes in here until we've cleaned up. Everyone else, you need full biohazard gear. I don't want any one exposed to whatever that is. Someone turn on the hose, so I can wash my hands before I touch anything or anyone. And Andrew, I know it's got to be hard, but resist the urge to kick what's left of her."

Teddy Bear

Senior Agent Jo Burns entered the coffee shop, looked around, and saw her cousin, Gavin, waiting for her.

After the normal greetings, Jo asked how his paranormal investigations business was going, as she suspected his request to grab lunch together probably related to that.

"Have you heard of possessed toys?" Gavin asked.

"Like Annabelle or Chucky? Yes, I've seen the movies."

"I mean in real life."

"You have got to be kidding me."

"No. It's a teddy bear. Everyone who has ever owned it has died, and my client inherited it, and she's scared. It doesn't give off any electromagnetic radiation, none of the tests I've tried showed anything, but still, it's been in her family for generations and everyone whose had it has died."

"Maybe she should throw it away."

"She would, but she's worried that someone might pick it up at the dump or something, you know, antique toys are worth money."

"So what did all of the people who owned it die of?"

"No-one knows. It goes back generations. People reached about forty and died. My client's thirty-five, and she just inherited the bear from her brother."

"What symptoms did the family members have before death?"

"None. Just some time in their forties, they'd just not wake up in the morning."

"Did this happen to any family members who did not have the bear?

"What?"

"Did any family members who didn't have the bear die in this manner?"

"I don't think so. I mean, I don't know. The client never said, but she's scared. Her brother's funeral is tomorrow, and then she has to clean up his house, and she has to do something with the bear."

"OK. Here's what I need to do. I need the bear to look at, and my pathologist will want to look at both your client, and her brother's body. If we can't find answers, I recommend she put the bear in her brother's coffin."

Back at the office, Jo inspected the bear.

"Anything wrong with this bear?" She asked the ghost of her daughter, Katie.

"It's old and a bit squished out of shape," Katie said.

"No ghosts, or spirits or demons?"

"No. Silly Mummy. It's just an old bear."

"That's what I thought, since I couldn't see anything. Let's see what Marissa has."

Agent Marissa Tyler had searched the family tree of Gavin's client.

"You were right," Marissa said. "Lots of people dropping dead for unknown reasons, for generations, and they can't all have had the bear. It follows back through her mother's family for generations, as far back as I was able to track."

"Then Helen will have the key, I'm sure."

It was not long before Pathologist Helen Thompson had something to report.

"This family hasn't just been handing a teddy bear down through the generations," Helen said. "They've also been sharing a genetic time bomb, long QT. It's a conduction disorder, messes with the electrical impulses in the heart. I'm

175

surprised it wasn't diagnosed, earlier, but it seems this family shares a form that doesn't display the normal warning symptoms, just one day the heart basically forgets to beat."

"I wondered if it might be something like that," Jo said. "Gavin's going to be disappointed he didn't get to defeat a demonic bear."

"But he may have, or we may have, just saved his client's life. That's got to be worth something."

"She's going to be all right?"

"There's medications, pacemakers if needed. There's no guarantees, of course, but a diagnosis is the first step. I've referred her to someone, and told her to notify her family members. There could be a lot of lives saved, or prolonged to normal length, since everyone dies." She paused a moment, and said, "Or rather, since almost everyone dies."

Jo met Gavin at the coffee shop once more.

"Since the bear's innocent, you can give it back," Jo said, handing the bear across the table.

"I heard about the results. My client is really thankful to your pathologist. She still paid me, even though there was nothing paranormal happening. She said it was still worth me getting involved since I knew who to ask."

"Well, by calling me, you did save her life."

"Yes, so I have another question."

"OK, what is it?"

"You know that possessed video in that movie The Ring? Could that happen in real life?"

"Highly unlikely."

"Good to know."

The teddy bear was sitting beside Gavin, so he didn't notice when it winked. Jo glared, not at the bear, but at the little ghost girl standing behind it. Katie giggled.

Kidnapper

Senior Agent Jo Burns parked her car in the carport, got out, opened the boot, took out two bags of groceries, closed the boot and started walking toward the house.

After being attacked here twice, she might have been more alert, except those attacks happened at night, and this was day time.

Her attention had been taken by the small girl in the Red Riding Hood costume, who was skipping and singing beside her. The ghost of her daughter Katie might have warned Jo, but she had been thinking about her favourite song, and how good it was her mother could see her now.

Jo felt the gun pressed into her back. She stood still.

"Seriously?" She said, "Is there some website or notice board, where every crook, crank, crazy, or generally dodgy bugger can find my home address?"

A male voice behind her said, "You're that cop's wife?"

"If you mean Inspector David Webber, it's ex-wife. We're divorced."

"You and I are going to walk into your house, and call your husband. Then I'm staying with you until he's done me a little favour."

"No."

"What do you mean, 'No?' I've got a gun."

"And you really shouldn't. You know it's illegal to carry a handgun and threaten people with it. That gun should be licensed, and kept in a locked gun safe, preferably at a gun club, so you're not carrying it around from place to place."

"What can I say? I like living on the edge. Now move, into the house."

"No."

"If you don't go I'm going to shoot you."

Katie was looking between her mother and the man, and giggling.

"Please don't shoot me. I like this blouse, and would hate to have it ruined. Why don't you just run along now. Leave the gun, I'll have it disposed of properly for you, wouldn't want it getting into the wrong hands."

He snarled, "It's already in the wrong hands, sweetheart. Now, like I said, walk."

"No."

"Walk, or I'll shoot you."

"That would be a mistake, a serious mistake."

"Walk, or I'll shoot you."

"You're very repetitive. I'm not letting you inside my house."

"I'm not afraid to shoot you."

"You really ought to be."

"Should I go and tell Kate?" Katie asked. It was near the full moon, so Agent Kate Murdoch would be able to see the ghost.

Jo said, "That's a good idea."

"What's a good idea?" The man asked.

Katie vanished.

"I wasn't talking to you," Jo answered.

The man's voice sounded a little nervous as he said, "Who are you talking to, then? Are you wearing a hidden microphone?"

Jo briefly considered ending the situation the quicker way. If she fought, however, the man might fire the gun, and the sound of gunshots could cause panic in suburban Brisbane. There was also a risk that in a fight, a bullet might harm someone walking past, or someone in a neighbouring house.

Jo didn't confirm or deny a hidden microphone. She said, "I've got back-up coming now. Do you want to wait here for them, or just leave?"

"Back up. What back up do you have? You just said you're not married to the cop any more."

Katie was back. She said: "Kate called Daddy. They said same plan as for Mrs X."

Jo nodded. David was coming along with Jo's team. She said to the man, "You found out where I live, but didn't find out what I do for a living?"

"You're a cop too?"

"Something like that."

"Then I don't even need your husband."

"Ex-husband."

"You can get me what I need."

"No."

"There's something of mine in your evidence locker."

"Not happening."

"Just get me my product, and I'll leave you alone."

"How about we skip the whole getting you your product part, and you just leave me alone?" She would keep him talking, give the team time to take position. Her team added danger, in that they were vulnerable to bullets, but, as they would come armed, there was also a good chance, they could persuade the man to surrender without shots being fired.

"Not happening, sweetheart."

"So, since we're standing here chatting, what's your name?"

"Do you think I'm an idiot?"

"I won't answer that. I don't want to hurt your feelings. So how does your plan to have me go and get your property work? You drive me to the police station, I walk in, then a station full of cops come out and arrest you?"

"Hmm. You're right. Back to the original plan. You're staying here with me, and your husband retrieves my property."

"Ex-husband. What makes you think he would care if you shot me? I can assure you, he really wouldn't be bothered by it at all."

In her peripheral vision, Jo could see her team moving in.

She heard David's voice: "Drop the gun. Put your hands over your head. Then turn around."

That was when the man made the worst possible decision in the situation. He squeezed the trigger on his gun.

Jo felt the bullet, a sudden, mild pressure against her impenetrable skin. There was no "bang", just a soft "thunk" as the bullet didn't leave the barrel of the gun that was pressed right against Jo's body.

The man felt the jolt of the gun's recoil, but still managed to hold it against Jo. Not understanding what was happening, he squeezed the trigger a second time. The second bullet struck the first, and the barrel of the gun exploded in his hand, causing severe burns and broken bones.

He screamed.

Jo's team moved in, and David arrested the man, before calling an ambulance for him.

Jo looked at the injured man and said, "Didn't I tell you I really liked this blouse?"

He looked at her, his face ashen, asked, "What are you?"

Jo smiled. She lowered both the pitch and volume of her voice, as she said, "I'm the reason you're giving up crime, because if you don't, I'll find you. You see my team here? They're not all completely human, either. They're keeping an eye on you, too."

Jo's team dispersed. Other police officers arrived at the same time as the ambulance, and David tasked them with accompanying the prisoner, as he would stay to get the victim's statement.

The ambulance and police car left.

David took Jo's groceries, while she unlocked the front door.

David said, "This might have been a good thing to have had a premonition about."

"I wish I could control that," she said. "There's one thing I can control, though. I really need to get a house with an attached garage."

"I thought you said you'd never leave this house."

"Because it's where all my memories of Katie were. Except, I have Katie with me wherever I go, now."

"If you want to sell, I'll buy this house … for the memories, since I can't see her."

Katie hugged her father. He smiled at the odd feeling he now knew meant she was touching him.

Pyotr

Pyotr Yefimovich swirled the deep red liquid in a crystal wine glass.

He wore his black hair slicked back, and dressed in a dinner suit and cloak. He'd adopted the garb in the 1950s, when he'd seen his first movie vampire, shedding his Russian peasant clothes. He had not seen fit to change his mode of dress since then.

He sipped slowly, savouring. AB negative was his favourite blood type, made more exclusive by its rarity. Not only was it the right type, but it was also the right age.

He asked his servant, "This beast, how old?"

Igor bowed slightly, "Nineteen, Master."

"This was from the new shipment?"

"Yes, Master."

"Transfer this one to my private stable. Add the oldest from my stable to the lot for on shipping to the client."

"As you wish, Master."

"Now, about our expansion plans. How soon can we move?"

"Master, I recommend not moving to Brisbane. You can still move into Australia, it's a large country, large enough to harvest many beasts, and to find many new clients. But choose another city, another state."

"I gather you've found out more about this Joanne Burns. Is she more than a mere legend?"

"More than legend, Master, and more than human."

"One of us?"

"Lazarai, of the clan Van Helsing."

"We've handled their type before."

"My sources say she has a spirit guardian, a ghost that always accompanies her, and helps protect her."

"A Van Helsing so weak she needs a guardian?"

"Not just the ghost, but she also has a team of humans and other beings. She has trained them and they are very effective at their work."

"They have not battled anyone as powerful as me."

"But, my Lord, they have. Jo Burns killed your cousin the Countess Anastasia Arafami, and two ancient ones who worked for her."

"None of us are ever truly dead."

"She destroyed their bloodstones. She despatches ancient vampires as easily as we kill humans. They are truly dead, beyond any help we could give."

Pyotr looked, thoughtfully, at the bracelet around his left wrist. It was made up of five large, deep red, stones, linked together with a delicate gold filigree. He said, "Igor, I am a firm believer in the adage that one must keep their friends close and their enemies closer. You know who the first stone on my bracelet is? The one I initially had in a gold ring?"

"Your brother, Master."

"My brother, Grigori Yefimovich Rasputin. I had warned him not to attract so much attention from the cattle. In the end they attempted to kill him at least three times. Eventually, I had to do it myself, to keep our existence secret. Do you know their historians are still trying to learn more about his early life? They're looking in the wrong century."

Igor felt he was meant to say something at this point. "Indeed, Master."

"I think I will want to have this Joanne Burns very close indeed."

"I really must advise against that, Master."

"Must you? You're becoming very tiresome, Igor. I'm happy to enlarge my bracelet if necessary."

"I apologise, Master. I am only doing what you employ me to do, giving you information and advice as you request."

"How many outposts does our enterprise have, now, Igor?"

"Twenty, in eleven different countries."

"And none yet in Australia. I think we must go there personally, to establish ourselves there, Igor. We must go to Brisbane, and establish an outpost. We must begin to trap wild cattle for sale on our international market."

"But Master, you've organised everything from Paris for so long. Why would you leave the comforts of home and go to this strange place. Sasha could go."

"Sasha will stay to manage the local business. We will control everything from Brisbane. Now, you will get us whatever travel papers we need, and arrange to purchase a suitable home there."

"Travel papers have changed since you moved from Siberia. You will need photographic proof of identification, to get the passport, which will itself be photographic proof of identification. You will need a regular bank account, not simply the numbered Swiss accounts."

"Are you saying you are unable to do this?"

"I'm saying it will take a significant amount of time and money."

"Do it."

Jo felt slightly light-headed as the premonition ended. She looked around at her office, her efficiently tidy desk, her ghost daughter in the corner, listening to the fairy tale Jo had set to play for her on an iPad. The story was only ten minutes long, and was still at the very beginning. Jo had been lost in the premonition for a minute or two at most, although it felt like a much longer time.

She had no idea if what she'd seen was happening at the time she saw it, or if would happen in the future. There'd been nothing to judge time or date from.

She phoned her second in charge, Agent Marissa Tyler, and told her: "Call a meeting. Get everyone in the conference room as soon as possible, David included. Something's coming. It's something worse than we've ever faced before."

"Vampire?"

"Ancient psycho vampire entrepreneur. He traffics human beings internationally for blood, and carries bloodstones from other vampires around on a bracelet, and he's related to the Countess, so he's got an axe to grind."

"I'll have everyone in the conference room in an hour."

"And I'll call my Uncle Kev. We might need outside help."

Opal

Senior Agent Jo Burnes sat at the coffee shop table. She said, "I don't have much time, Gavin, We've got something big happening at work."

Her cousin Gavin said, "I'll be quick. I need advice on this."

He took something wrapped in cloth out of his backpack. The item was the size of a football. As soon as the item left his back back, a ghost appeared behind him. The ghost was a man, apparently in his late forties, in dusty clothes and an Akubra hat.

Gavin unwrapped the item. It was a massive opal.

Jo looked at it and glanced up at the ghost, which was invisible to everyone else in the coffee shop.

"It's cursed," Gavin said.

"Cursed? You mean like the Hope Diamond, or the Koh I Nor?"

"My client's father Charlie and his friend Darren were opal miners together. They found this. It's the biggest opal ever mined in Australia."

"And one of them died?" Jo looked at the ghost.

"Both of them died. As they dug it out, the mine caved in killing Darren. Charlie barely got out with his life."

"But he managed to drag out a massive opal while barely getting out?" Jo was already suspicious of the story Gavin was telling.

The ghost said, "Charlie took the stone out. I was still back there, digging further into the seam. He set off dynamite to trap me and then left me there to die."

Jo nodded. She told Gavin about the ghost behind him and what had been said. Gavin looked over his shoulder nervously.

"Should we do an exorcism or something?" Gavin asked.

"How about you go on with the story?"

Charlie took the opal to jeweller to cut it and polish it. A week later, the jeweller had a massive heart attack and died."

Jo looked at the ghost who shrugged. She said to Gavin, "By any chance was the jeweller old, or overweight, or alcoholic, or a smoker, or something like that?"

Gavin pulled out a folder and found the death certificate, he said, "Ah yes, a pre-existing cardiac condition."

Jo nodded.

"Anyway, Charlie put the opal in an auction, expecting it would get a lot of money. It was advertised as the Peacock Tail Opal because of the colours in it. The auction house accepted it, but before the auction they gave it back to Charlie, and said they wouldn't sell it. They claimed all of their staff had nightmares about the stone, and about being trapped in a mine or cave or somewhere underground. "

Jo looked at the ghost, and said, "I guess that was you?"

The ghost nodded, and said, "I don't have any other way to talk to people, well, most people."

Jo asked, "And what were you trying to tell them? That Charlie had murdered you?"

"That and that, the opal should have been half mine, and he was going to keep all of the money. My wife and kids need my share."

Jo told Gavin what the ghost had said. Then asked, "What happened next?"

Gavin said, "So Charlie had to go to Sydney to drop the opal off with the auction house, and then to pick it up again.

He went back to his hotel room, got drunk, and fell over the room's balcony, three storeys onto concrete. So his daughter, my client, inherited the cursed opal."

The ghost said, "I may have given him a slight push. I didn't actually realise I could affect him, though."

Jo thought a moment and asked the ghost, "So what's your end goal here? What do you want?"

The ghost replied, "I want my family to get my share of the proceeds of the sale."

Jo told this to Gavin. She suggested he ring the client while she was there to talk with Darren's ghost.

Gavin made the call. His client agreed.

Jo looked over Gavin's shoulder at the ghost, and asked, "Are you good with that."

The ghost agreed that was all that he wanted, then he disappeared in a wisp of smoke.

Jo said, "Well, that's his unfinished business settled and he's gone. As long as your client keeps her promise, there shouldn't be any more problems. So with this paranormal investigations business, do you actually do any of your own work?"

Gavin blushed, and said, "I'm available to help you with your work, too."

"Good to know."

At home that night, Jo began to wonder what unfinished business was keeping her daughter Katie's ghost around.

She asked, "Katie, is there something making you unhappy? Is that why you stay here?"

Katie giggled. "No Mummy. Something makes me very happy. That's being with you and with Daddy. I'm very, very, happy you can see me now. I don't want to go away."

"If something did make you sad, you would tell me, wouldn't you?"

"Of course, Mummy."

Vampire Watch

Senior Agent Jo Burns was having a premonition.

It was a large room, with a window overlooking a river. There was mahogany desk on one side of the room, with a large mahogany, red-velvet upholstered arm chair, that looked more like a throne pulled up to it. In front of the desk, were two more similar arm chairs. The walls were lined with empty bookshelves, with cardboard boxes on the floor beside them. One of the boxes was open, revealing it was packed with books.

Standing in the doorway was the vampire Jo knew from a previous vision as Igor. Igor was looking frightened, as he gave his master some extremely bad news.

"I'm sorry, Master. None of the vampires here will buy our product. They say this Jo Burns arranged for them to have the blood they need, so they will not buy cattle from us. They are afraid of her, and will not go against her rules. They would rather live among the cattle, than take their rightful place as rulers."

"That's not good enough, Igor," his master, Pyotr, responded.

"Master, I have tried. They will not be moved. They will not buy from us, and they will not work for us."

"The trade only works if we have customers, and workers to capture and transport the product."

"Yes, Master."

"So you know what we must do."

"Yes, Master."

"What?"

"Master?"

"What must we do, Igor?"

"I don't know, Master. I only know that you know."

"Then why did you say 'yes'?"

"Because if I said 'no', you would hurt me, Master."

"What we have to do is to kill this Joanne Burns, and those of our own kind who refuse to join us. Then we must create new vampires, new workers, and new customers."

"Yes, Master. But, Master…"

"But what, Igor?"

Jo lost the vision. As before she didn't know if she'd seen something currently happening, or something that would happen in the future.

Before Jo could reflect on the vision and what she'd learned from it, her phone rang.

A voice male voice said, "Is that Agent Burns."

She answered, "Yes, it is. Can I help you?"

"You don't know me. Well, I don't think you know me. I'm Brendan Curtis. I'm a vampire. I arrived here during the Countess' time, but I wasn't one of the vampires created by her."

"Go on."

"There's this guy in town. He has, I don't know, an Eastern European accent, I think. He's been tracking down all the vampires, and trying to sell us humans, for blood. He calls humans cattle. I told him, everyone told him, about our deal. The deal you organised. We get our blood from the blood bank. Some of us, those of us who can, give them cash donations in return, because even humans buy their food, so it's only fair."

"So no-one's taking his offer."

"No-one. We've all been talking to each other. We like the system we've got, but we all thought you should know about this."

"This vampire who approached you, was his name Igor?"

"Yes. Has someone else told you about him?"

"I have some intelligence about him. He works for someone very powerful, who doesn't like to hear the word no."

"We're forming our own Neighbourhood Watch, like the wolves have. We'll watch each other's backs, and I'll let you know anything we hear. If you want to contact us, I can pass any messages on."

"Do you know where Igor and Pyotr are living?"

"No, but if I hear, I'll call you."

"Thanks. And if my team or I learn anything that can help keep you safe, we'll let you know. We still don't know how to find these two, but I have some experts coming in to help. We don't have a vampire on the team here currently, but if you like, I can get someone to act as liaison between the HDU and the Vampire Watch."

"Yes, I think we'd all appreciate that."

"This number you called me on, is that the best to contact you?"

"Yes."

"Then I'll have Marissa Tyler call you later today."

Jo hung up the phone.

Kev Burns and Andrea Domichi from the Van Helsing clan were due to arrive at the airport in an hour. With their expertise, and her team, she hoped it would be possible to kill Pyotr, before he could start his plans for her city.

Sharing Information

Senior Agent Jo Burns, her second-in-command Agent Marissa Tyler, and the Van Helsing clan members Kev Burns, and Andrea Domichi sat around the table in the meeting room at the Human Defence Unit offices.

Kev said, "It's bad. I've checked our records. Jo, I'll show you how to access them later. The Van Helsings have had contact with Pyotr before, and it hasn't gone well for our people. He's been running his human trafficking business for centuries. He's also skilled at compulsion."

Jo said, "Compulsion?"

Kev said, "You've read Dracula?"

Jo nodded.

"Compulsion is like hypnosis. Some ancient vampires are very good at it. Pyotr is one. It's understood his brother, Grigori, was as well. People who have been bitten by a vampire and not turned, or recovered, are exceptionally vulnerable. I understand when you killed the Countess and her sidekicks, a lot of people were returned to their human form. They're especially vulnerable to compulsion."

Marissa and Jo exchanged a meaningful glance.

Kev said, "What don't I know?"

Jo explained, "One of our former agents, Harry had been turned by the Countess. He became human again when we killed the Countess. He didn't adapt well to being human again. He took her bloodstone from my desk, and raised her, and had her turn him once more. While they were trying to escape, he bit Marissa. She killed him while he was biting her, so she didn't actually turn, but she was severely injured."

Marissa moved the collar of her shirt to reveal the huge scar on her neck.

Jo continued, "After that, we were able to kill the Countess again, and I destroyed her bloodstone. So not only was the vampire who attacked her killed, but his creator was as well. Are you saying she's now particularly vulnerable to this compulsion?"

"I'm afraid I am."

Marissa said, "I'm also the liaison with the new Vampire Watch. They're counting on me to help keep them safe, and they're taking the risk of passing on any information they receive to us, so it's important we help protect them."

Andrea shook her head. She said, "This is the first time I've seen vampire hunters who helped protect vampires."

"We protect humans," Jo said. "That doesn't mean we have to kill beings that are choosing not to harm humans. We've helped arrange a system to get them the blood they need without being a threat to humans. As long as they're not a threat, we're happy to work with them. So are our local vampires also at risk of compulsion, or is it only humans who have been bitten?"

Kev said, "Pyotr is ancient enough, and proficient enough in his skills that he could probably influence younger or weak-willed vampires, or even humans who haven't been bitten. Humans who have been bitten are more vulnerable, but they're not the only ones who can be effected."

Jo asked the obvious question, "How about us? Lazarai in general, and Van Helsing clan in particular?"

Kev said, "Those of us in this room, unlikely. We're all too strong willed. But others have been effected in the past. I understand that was Pyotr and Grigori working together, so he may not be strong enough on his own."

"He has Grigori with him. I saw it in a vision. He wears five bloodstones on a bracelet, and he said the first one was his brother. He can get Grigori back any time he wants him," Jo said.

Ken was quiet for a moment, absorbing the news. Then he said, "I don't know what to say. Five more ancient vampires, old enough to leave bloodstones, makes thing entirely more complicated. You can add to that, neither Andrea nor I have had any visions of him, but you've said he talked about you in both your visions of him. Our working theory is that his thinking about you has opened him up more to you seeing him, which would mean your visions of him were real time, not the future. That confirms he is here, although your intelligence from the local vampires tells you that anyway. If only we had a way to make him think about you more often."

Marissa said, "I can help with that. I'll tell the Vampire Watch, that any time Igor or Pyotr himself approaches them, they should mention Jo. I'd also suggest we contact every former vampire we know of from the Countess' community, and make sure they've all got Jo's business card, warn them about Pyotr's skills and encourage them to call her if anything strange happens, so we'll have them thinking of her, perhaps talking about her."

Andrea nodded, and said, "That's a pretty good idea. I wonder if there's any other way we keep Jo front and centre in his mind."

"We need to keep thinking about that. We also, urgently need to find a way to locate him. What do you know so far?" Kev asked.

Jo thought, "I saw a large window, overlooking the river. The room looked really big, and was really richly furnished."

Kev said, "We know from the records, that he buys mansions wherever he lives. Does that help narrow it down?"

Jo shook her head. "Not really, a lot of the houses along the river are pretty big, and expensive. And it's a big river, with a lot of suburbs along both sides."

Kev said, "Well, we start by contacting all of those beings Marissa mentioned, to have them mention Jo if approached.

We can pull pictures of Pyotr and Igor from our files, to circulate to those contacts in case they see them."

Jo said, "If there's pictures, we can give them to David to circulate around all of the local police stations. He can say they're wanted in relation to human trafficking charges, which is completely true. If that's all we can do for now, I suggest, Marissa and I get on to our contacts, and the two of you can check into your hotel."

Before leaving the HDU office, Kev asked Jo to call up the Lazarus family tree he'd given her the link to before. He showed her a symbol of a blood drop in the top right corner, and told her to click it. That took her to a menu which gave her access to all of the Van Helsing clan's files. He told her if she had clicked a small cross in the top left corner, it would have taken her to historic documentation of all of the Lazarai aid work. A coin in the bottom left corner led to a list of all current and past businesses owned by Lazarus Corp. A tree on the bottom left corner was for the family tree page. The four symbols appeared on every page, so it was possible to go to any section of the site.

Jo asked, "Can just anyone access this?"

Kev laughed, "Anyone with access to this very particular corner of the web, who has been pre-approved. It's not even dark web. It's completely our own. Believe me, only people Lazarus has personally authorised can get into this. No passwords needed, the site knows if you are or are not approved."

"That's some pretty advanced tech."

"That's a pretty advanced combination of Lazarus' own powers with tech. He wasn't even satisfied with making it available to all Lazarai. He realised that just being one of us didn't necessarily make a person trustworthy, although he personally created each one of us. As far as I know none of us have ever betrayed him, or the community, but he did have a big experience of betrayal way back. So he wanted to be able to withdraw someone's access if it was ever necessary."

Kev went on to show Jo how to add her own reports to the Van Helsing files.

Jo, thinking about now being part of two secret organisations, said, "Lazarus knows, doesn't he, that if it was a choice, I would choose the HDU over the Lazarai?"

"Lazarus knows your integrity. He knows you would always choose what you believe is right. There's a reason he told us to always report to you if we were in your city."

"Fair enough."

Compulsion

Agent Marissa Tyler attended a small meeting of members of the Vampire Watch, in the home of the Watch leader, Brendan Curtis. The meeting was at night, as most of the members weren't old enough vampires to survive daylight.

Marissa told the group everything the HDU knew about the Vampire Pyotr, and his assistant, Igor. She suggested that if one of these vampires approach them, to mention Senior Agent Jo Burns and the program she had helped develop which provided vampires blood from the blood bank. She also asked them to take note of any information which might help the HDU to find them.

"Basically, these guys want to recruit you all, or create new vampires. They want workers, and customers for their human trafficking ring. I understand no-one here is planning on getting involved with them. If anyone does, that will create issues with the HDU, and will interfere with the current relationship we have."

A woman who had been quiet for most of the evening said, "I know where they're living. I mean, I know somewhere they've been. I don't know for sure they're still there. After Igor approached me, I followed him home. I knew if he was trying to stir things up, someone would want to know about him. So that's why I followed him. He went to one of those huge riverside houses in Yeronga. None of us live there, so I guessed that's where they live."

Marissa got the address.

When the meeting broke up, she texted the information to Jo, and said she would meet her there.

Marissa drove to the street, and parked a couple of houses down. She walked back along the footpath, saw the front gate of the house was open, and let herself into the front yard. Seeing movement in one of the front windows, she moved in closer, hiding herself behind a hedge. She did not notice that the woman vampire who had given her the address had followed her, and was hiding behind a tree.

Marissa could clearly see in the room, a tall man in a long cloak and top hat. Jo had said Pyotr had styled himself along the lines of old movie vampires. There he was, pacing up and down the room, the cloak swirling each time he turned. He seemed to be talking animatedly to someone who was sitting in the shadows out of her sight.

Suddenly, Pyotr stopped mid turn. He looked directly at Marissa through the window.She was sure he couldn't see her behind the hedge, but still, could see his eyes glowing, staring, as if he were looking right into the deepest part of her mind. A cold feeling came over her. She could hear the voice in her head, a male voice with a pronounced Eastern European accent. It was a strange voice, firm and confident, but deep and quiet. This was a man who never had to raise his voice to be obeyed. His voice sounded almost musical.

He said, "Marissa Tyler. Marissa, my sweet, my beloved. You belong with me, but Joanne Burns is keeping us apart. You must kill Joanne Burns, so we can be together, you and I. We belong together, but Joanne Burns is preventing that. Kill her, then come to me."

Jo came back to herself, and narrowly avoided a collision. She'd had the vision while driving. She was shocked, by both her near miss, and by the possibility that Marissa might try to harm her.

"You OK boss?" Agent Kate Murdoch asked from the passenger seat.

"New plan," Jo said. "Have you got a tranquilliser gun with you?"

"No, I thought it was just crossbows and wooden bolts. I mean even UV isn't going to do much against an ancient vampire."

"Check the glove box. I keep a tranq gun in there for emergencies. Pyotr's using compulsion on Marissa. I want you to tranq her as soon as we arrive, to keep her out of harm's way. Call the others, and let them know. And tell them we all have to watch each other for signs that anyone's been influenced."

Kate called Kev Burns, who was in another car with his hunting partner Andrea Domichi, and Agent Elizabeth Jones, who was in a third vehicle with Agent Scott Cooper.

They all parked a block away from the house, and walked, from different directions. A small ghost girl, in a Red Riding Hood costume, skipped along beside Jo.

Approaching the house, they could see Marissa watching through the window.

"I'll go first," Kate said. "So she doesn't see you before I can tranq her."

Jo nodded.

Kate walked up behind Marissa.

The little ghost of Jo's daughter Katie called out, "Mummy, behind them!"

Jo saw a vampire stepping into view coming up behind Kate, as she sneaked up behind Marissa.

Jo fired a crossbow at the same instant as Kate fired the tranq gun.

The female vampire and Marissa both went down, as the other agents and the two Van Helsing vampire hunters arrived.

"He's got to know we're here," Jo whispered. "That wasn't quiet enough for vampire hearing to miss it. So I'm smashing this big window here, and entering this way. Kate, you're with me, watch my back. Kev, and Andrea, can you both split up? You can both see Katie, we've found she's a good way to send quick and quiet messages before. So if one of you could go with Scott and one with Elizabeth, that would help. Each pair, find another way to access the house. Don't worry about property damage breaking in, just get in there, and we search until we find them, and we kill them.

The house was dark. The team turned on light switches as they entered rooms. Vampires could see in the dark. Humans could not.

Kev and Elizabeth found Igor hiding in a wardrobe on the first floor. Elizabeth despatched him with a crossbow bolt. When he disintegrated to ash, She kicked through it, and found the bloodstone, which she ground under the heel of her boot.

Kev watched approvingly. "You destroy the bloodstones?"

Elizabeth said, "Something I learned from Jo. She always makes sure they can't come back. She'll make us cremate that one in the front yard later, since it was young and didn't decompose. I sometimes miss working in Sydney, but I've learned so much more, working here."

Jo and Kate found Pyotr in the library, sitting in a large armchair, sipping blood from a wine glass.

"I saw you knew your friend was going to attack you," he said, calmly. "You took evasive action. I'm quite impressed with you, Ms Burns."

Jo smiled, "When someone tries to make my friend kill me, I take it personally. So I'm sure you'll understand why I'm going to kill you."

"That friend of yours was particularly susceptible, but I can compel ordinary humans." He stared at Kate. "Kill her. You know you want to," he said, in his low, hypnotic voice.

Kate shook her head, and said, "No. I don't really want to ... and I'm not human."

Jo and Kate both raised their crossbows and fired. Both bolts pierced his heart.

He disintegrated to dust.

Jo bent over and searched through the dust, and found both Pyotr's bloodstone, and the bracelet with five similar stones on it. She took out her service weapon, and with six shots, destroyed all of the stones.

Katie flitted from group to group, giving updates.

In the front yard, Jo gave instructions for the cremation of the younger vampire, and for getting Marissa back to headquarters and placed in the care of their pathologist Helen Thompson.

Jo asked Kev, "Will she be OK? Does the compulsion wear off?"

"Even if it didn't otherwise, killing Pyotr should have ended it."

"Oh good. I mean she's got to get back to the Vampire Watch with the news." She sighed and said, "One day we should have a family reunion that doesn't involve killing anything."

"Killing stuff's in our blood."

"I should tell that to Gavin. He's my cousin, your great-great nephew."

"Is he in the business, too?"

"He's a paranormal investigator."

"Any good?"

"He hasn't discovered Katie yet."

"Genetics. Sometimes it's hit and miss."

They followed the others away from the mansion, leaving all of the lights on, as the darkness of the night deepened.